ONLY FOR A MOMENT

The McCormicks
Book 2

ELENA AITKEN

Chapter One

MITCH

THE BOAT CUT through the gentle waves of the lake, smooth and easy. I grinned and pressed down on the accelerator, urging the boat to move faster still. I knew I was pushing it. The engine was brand-new and my brother had given me explicit instructions to "warm up the boat gently."

"Screw gently."

I pushed further and with a satisfying roar of the engine, the boat surged forward. The wind blew my hair back from my face. I tilted my head up to the sun and let out a yell. It was these moments, when I could steal away from Dockside—my brother's brand-new marina—to enjoy the fresh mountain air on my own, that I truly felt free.

I hadn't even been back in Cedar Springs a full month, but it didn't matter. I was home. It was funny how the tiny town in the middle of the mountains where I'd spent my summers as a kid had always been more home than any other. Maybe it was because we had so many great memories there as a family. Maybe it was because those summers had been when I'd really grown up. But maybe it was just because there was no place quite as wild and open to possibility as the middle of a mountain lake on a hot summer day.

Not that it mattered. It was only the beginning of July, and even if I did have to return to the city and the pretentious private school where I worked, I was at least going to have the summer to enjoy myself.

I was about to push the throttle even further when my cell phone vibrated in my pocket.

Ian.

I laughed and shook my head before I slowed the boat and answered the call. "You have a tracker on me?"

"Should I?"

"No." I stifled my laughter. "Not at all. What's up?"

I knew exactly what was up. The Canada Day celebration was that night and Ian was going crazy with his share of the preparations. As the new business owner in town, and the first summer of the Dockside being open, it was important that they do a good job with their assigned duties. Which, as far as I could tell, only involved helping to haul the barge out into the lake, where the fireworks would be set off.

"When were you planning on getting back here with my new investment?"

Ahh. It wasn't about the celebrations at all, but Ian's precious new boat. Not that I could blame him. My big brother had sunk a lot of money into the Dockside, an investment that seemed to be paying off as the town became a bigger tourist attraction than it had ever been. But still, there must be stress associated with it all.

Not that I had any idea. I was simply a schoolteacher on a break from my life.

"Simmer down. I'm on my way back." Just so I wasn't lying, I steered the boat around and started to head back, very slowly, in the direction of the marina. "I'll take good care of your baby. What's the hurry, anyway?"

"I need to get to a meeting."

There it was. The real reason for the call.

"I'm on my way. I'll be there in five. Three if you let me open 'er up."

"Five is fine." I could almost see Ian rolling his eyes. "Drive easy. It's a new engine. You have to warm it up."

"Leave it to me, brother. I got this." I disconnected the call and put the boat into gear.

Ever since Ian and his fiancée Gwen had signed the contract to have Gwen's social media posts, and subsequently, their love story, turned into a television show, there'd been a never ending stream of meetings, phone calls, emails, and all types of distractions for Ian, which left me to take care of the main operations of Dockside for the last few weeks. Not that I minded. It gave me something to do to distract me from everything I'd left back in the city. Or mainly, whom I'd left in the city. Not that she was worth too much of my mental energy.

Especially considering there had been other distractions, too. My lips curled up into a smile, thinking about what that particular distraction had been. And damn, it was definitely worth smiling about.

Jade Johnson.

Just thinking about the tall, sexy brunette made my dick twitch. Damn. From the moment Gwen's agent had showed up in town, I couldn't take my eyes off the woman. And although there'd definitely been a few perks to that, primarily the night of the summer solstice festival—a night I wasn't going to soon forget—there was also one major problem with Jade.

She was a stiletto-wearing, designer bag-toting, full-fledged, first-class, high-maintenance city girl.

The exact type of woman I usually avoided. No, scratch that; I usually ran screaming in the opposite direction. In my experience, and I'd certainly had my share, that type of woman was nothing but trouble. High maintenance, full on, drama type of trouble. Not only did they want to be wined and dined where only the best would do, they wanted it all the time. I knew that type. My bank account knew that type. And I'd emptied my wallet one too many times to fall for it again.

It wasn't just the money either. I'd never be able to take a city girl out in the boat, let the wind blast through her hair and the sun kiss her skin before having a picnic on the beach where they'd eat a healthy dose of sand with their lunch before making love with the waves of the lake licking their toes.

No. A "makeup just right, not a hair out of place" type of girl would definitely not go for that type of thing. And dammit, that's what I wanted.

It was a feeling that had surprised me, too. My brothers used to refer to me as a player, never with the same girl longer than a week. And for a long time, it was a title I'd deserved. For my entire adult life, the very last thing I wanted was to be tied down.

Until Bethany.

Maybe it was because she'd been my longest relationship. Maybe it was because she used to whisper to me about the future. Maybe it was because she'd wanted me just as much as I'd wanted her.

Whatever it was, Bethany had changed my view on commitment and settling down. I'd really thought she might be the one. At least until she'd slept with the principal at the school we both taught at.

That was definitely a game changer.

My experience with Bethany had absolutely changed the way I felt about her. But to my surprise, it hadn't changed how I now felt about commitment.

Seeing my big brother so happy with his own love had only fueled the want.

"Shit." I cursed under my breath. The boat ride was supposed to have cleared my head. The idea was to forget Bethany and women altogether, and strip my mind from any stress. Like a form of meditation. And most of the time it worked. But as I approached the shore and the marina appeared, the only thing I could do was curse.

My mind was definitely not clear.

I guided the boat into a stall, hopped out and easily tied it securely to a cleat before I jogged down the dock to the main office. Maybe busying myself with some work would help.

"Hey."

"Mitch!" Gwen pulled me into a tight hug before she leaned in to my ear. "It's about time you got back. Your brother is a total stress case about this meeting."

"Not to worry." I kissed my sister-in-law-to-be on the cheek and slid out of her grasp. I genuinely liked Gwen, and I was thankful she'd forgiven me the transgressions of my youth, which mostly involved calling her Giant Gigi when we were teenagers. Not that it was any kind of excuse, but ten years ago, Gwen didn't look anything like the stunning woman she'd grown into. After a massive weight loss, a new haircut, and some contact lenses, she was a totally different person.

Which was what she'd based her social media accounts on. She'd blown up earlier in the summer when Gwen exploited her past feelings for Ian and tricked him into a relationship. It was all pretty messed up, really, but when the truth came out, love won the day, and I couldn't be happier for both of them.

"Get out of here," I said to Ian, who was frantically typing into the laptop. "I can handle anything you have for the rest of the day. What needs to be done?"

I only half listened while Ian gave me the rundown on what needed to be done around the Dockside. Finally, my big brother was satisfied and ready to leave.

"Come on, Ian." Gwen tugged his arm. "I told Jade we'd be there five minutes ago."

"Jade?"

Gwen turned and raised an eyebrow in my direction.

"Jade's going to be there?" I was vaguely aware that I probably sounded like a moron, but damn, Jade was worth sounding at least a little foolish for. Especially if it meant the possibility of a repeat night like the one we'd shared only a few weeks ago.

"Of course she's going to be there." Gwen winked at me. "She's working on this with us, remember?"

As if I'd forgotten.

"Maybe I'll see her later." I shrugged and turned back to the laptop in an effort to play it cool. For a man who didn't want anything to do with a designer label chick, I sure wasn't doing a good job convincing anyone. Especially myself.

JADE

WE'D BEEN LOOKING at head shots and resumes all morning, and I was more than ready for a break. Not that I didn't enjoy spending my time looking at pictures of hot men; I did. But there was only so much one woman could take before she started getting a little hot under the collar herself. But it wasn't any of the men in the photos who were making me squirm in my seat in the vinyl booth at the Grizzly Paw.

It was one man.

One man who had only been one time and that's all it could ever be. One night.

Mitch McCormick was not the type of man I needed in my

life. Even if he was smoking hot in a strong, confident, just a little rough around the edges type of way.

Damn.

No. I mentally chastised myself. Mitch was a one-time thing only. I didn't need to get involved with his type. Or any type, for that matter. Just like my mother had always told me: "A man is good for one thing, and one thing only. Beyond that, if you want to make something of yourself, don't get attached. Never get attached."

And I did want to make something of myself. Now with Gwen and Ian's show taking off, things were finally starting to happen. I loved being an agent, and I wasn't giving that up, especially considering my clients were largely authors and didn't require a ton of hands-on work. But working on Mr. Summer was a huge opportunity. Not to mention, it would be fun and exciting. A man—especially a man like Mitch McCormick—would be nothing but an unnecessary distraction.

Besides that, I'd done pretty well in my life up until now with my mother's advice. Men may be good for one thing only, but some of those men were definitely better at that thing than others.

I felt my face flush at the memory of the way Mitch had slid his hands down my skin to cup my breasts and tease my nipples into hard points before pushing me up against the wall of the Dockside gift shop and—

"Jade?"

I snapped back to the present and the two people sitting across from me, currently staring at me as if I'd lost my mind.

"Are you okay?" Gwen slid a glass of water across the table. "You look a little flushed."

I took a controlled and practiced breath. I could feel my body temperature return to normal. I'd worked hard on my composure. It wasn't often I let it slip. Especially in a meeting.

To buy myself another minute, I took the offered water and had a sip, letting the cool liquid soothe me from the inside. Mitch definitely had an effect on me; there was no denying that.

"I'm fine, thank you," I said after a moment. "I think all these good-looking men are starting to blend into one another. How about we take a break?"

Ian groaned. "Can we just get this done? It's Canada Day, Jade. The picnic starts soon. I don't know why we had to have a meeting today anyway."

Gwen patted his arm and gave it a squeeze. I tried not to feel the twinge of jealousy at their happy coupling. Gwen had turned from client to friend, and although our friendship was still developing, I really was happy for them both. And not just because their relationship was the entire reason I currently found myself in Cedar Springs with a huge career opportunity. Although, it didn't hurt.

"Okay," I conceded. "We can wrap it up. But I really would like to at least narrow down some of the candidates for the lead roles." I gathered up the pile of photos in front of me and flipped through them again. "There's just no one here who really strikes me as a McCormick."

"What about an actual McCormick?"

Pictures forgotten, my head shot up. I stared at Ian, who grinned at me. "No." He waved his hand. "Not me. There's no way you'll get me in front of the camera. But what about my little brother, Cal?"

"Cal's an actor?" Gwen obviously didn't know anything about this idea either. "I thought he was a super famous model in Australia."

"He isn't," Ian said. "And he is."

I blinked and tried to focus as Ian handed me a picture of a very good-looking, very McCormick man.

"He is a model in Australia," Ian clarified. "And he hasn't

done any real acting work yet. Well, not beyond a few commercials. But he was looking to get into it and come home for a visit. It seems like a perfect opportunity."

He didn't have any experience? My immediate response was to say no. After all, taking a risk on an unproven actor could be risky. Then again, we were all new and unproven. None of us had ever written, produced, or even been involved with a television production before. So really, it probably couldn't hurt to give him a chance.

Especially if he was willing to work on our budget. Which wasn't much to speak of.

"He'd be willing to cut his teeth on this project? It's not a very big—"

"He knows all about the project," Ian said. "Including the lack of budget. It would be a pay cut from his modeling gigs, but he seems to be okay with that. Besides, it might be just the break he's looking for. After all, Mr. Summer is going to be the next big thing, right?" He looked to the ladies, and Gwen giggled.

But I was too busy letting the idea percolate. It could be a very clever marketing angle to have the actual brother of Mr. Summer playing him. And there was definitely a family resemblance.

In fact, the more I thought about it, the more I liked the idea.

"When can he get here?"

"Given that I just found out about it myself, I have no idea." Gwen shrugged. "But I'm willing to bet, Ian already told him to get on a plane." She looked at her fiancé. "Am I wrong?"

He grinned. It was the only answer we needed. "But I did tell him he'd still have to go through the screen test and script read and all that stuff. But I really do think he's a good fit."

If it meant not having to sift through any more head shots,

I was game to give it a try. "Now we need to come up with a female lead."

Ian tipped his beer bottle back and swallowed the last of his drink before sliding out of the booth. "I'll leave that to the ladies. I really need to check on a few things with the fireworks barge." He kissed Gwen on the forehead, which I knew was only for my benefit. If I hadn't been sitting there under some semblance of a business meeting, it likely would have turned into a heavy make-out session between the two of them. I felt that twinge of envy again, but quickly dismissed it.

The second Ian was out the door, Gwen's hands shot out and grabbed mine. She squeezed them tight, her eyes lit up with excitement. "Okay," she said. "Spill."

"What are you talking about?" I laughed nervously, because I was fairly sure I did know what Gwen was talking about, and I wasn't about to get into it.

"Oh, come on." She squeezed my hands one more time before she dropped them. "You and Mitch. What's going on? Talk. I want to know everything."

I swallowed hard. I wanted this; I wanted a girlfriend to confide things in. To share the giggles and secrets that good friends had. I couldn't remember ever having a close friend. I'd been too busy building my career; friendships were like relationships, just a liability on the path to success.

Gwen was the closest thing I had ever had for a real friend. It was sad really, because Gwen was a client. She was a client. Now we were colleagues. Now we could be friends. I looked across the table at the other woman, who was waiting for me to share some piece of information with her. Something that girlfriends would share.

"I don't really have—"

"Oh, come on." Gwen narrowed her eyes playfully. "I'm not blind. I saw the way the two of you looked at each other at the festival and pretty much every time you were in the room together before and since. The heat between the two of you is crazy. So, are you two dating or something? Mitch has been totally tight-lipped about it."

"He has?"

"Of course. 'Cause he's a man. And he's practically my brother-in-law, and…well, we're still working on our relationship."

I nodded thoughtfully. I knew all about the relationship between Gwen and Ian's younger brother. It hadn't been the most positive one when they were kids, and it was Mitch who'd recognized Gwen when he came to town and more or less outed her to Ian, which had caused all kinds of drama, only a few weeks earlier. All that seemed like a million years ago though because now everyone had made up and everything had worked out.

"Of course," I said. "But you're not kids anymore. I'm sure you guys will find your common ground soon."

"For sure we will." Gwen brushed it off. "And right now, I think that common ground is you."

I would have blushed if I were the blushing type. But I most certainly was not. I also was not the type to kiss and tell. Under normal circumstances, I would have kept my mouth shut about what had happened between me and Mitch at the festival.

But this wasn't normal.

This could quite possibly be the start of a real, genuine friendship.

"Okay, okay." I squeezed my eyes shut momentarily. "But you can't tell anyone."

"Ohh, this sounds good."

I could not believe I was doing this. Never in my whole life had I ever discussed a man with anyone. Not ever. I took a deep breath. "We kissed."

Gwen sat back in the booth as if she'd been smacked. Her mouth fell open. "You *kissed*?"

I nodded.

"And?"

"And what?" I didn't understand. Wasn't that exactly what Gwen wanted to hear? "We did."

"I'm sure you did." Gwen rolled her eyes. "And that's it?"

"Well…"

"Ah-ha!" Gwen shouted and pointed a finger at me gleefully. "I knew there was more. You guys totally hooked up, didn't you?"

Was this really happening? The last thing I needed was everyone in town knowing my business. I glanced around to see whether anyone was paying attention, but the few people who were in the bar all minded their own business and were in no way concerned with what the two women in the booth were talking about.

"Keep your voice down." I grabbed Gwen's hands and pressed them to the table. "I don't want everyone knowing!"

"So you did?" Gwen's voice really was way too loud.

"Gwen!"

"Sorry." The woman self-corrected and although her voice was lower, she practically bounced in her seat. "And? Was it amazing? I bet it was. You two clearly have chemistry. Anyone can see it. I knew the first time I saw you together, the two of you had sparks. Major sparks."

Was it amazing? Was it ever. Just remembering the way Mitch touched my body, his fingers leaving a streak of heat on my skin. The way his lips moved against my neck, my breasts, my— Oh yes, it had been amazing, all right. It was almost too bad it wouldn't happen again.

And I told my new friend as much. "It was a one-time thing."

"No way."

"Yes way."

"Well, that's just ridiculous." Gwen slapped both palms against the table and pushed up from the table. "I can see in your face that you don't believe that. And even if you do, I don't. But I have to run. I'll see you later at the picnic?"

"Of course." I smiled. Not because I was excited about a small-town picnic, but because I had been looking forward to the possibility of seeing Mitch again. Because Gwen was right: I kept telling myself that whatever happened between me and Mitch was a one-time thing, but I wasn't so sure anymore that I wanted it to be.

Chapter Two

MITCH

"YOU ARE ABSOLUTELY THE BEST." Chelsea stood on her tiptoes to plant a kiss on my cheek. "You really are, Mitch. Thank you so much."

I wasn't so convinced that I was the best, especially considering earlier, I'd spent more than a few minutes cursing my little sister when she'd called to convince me to cover for her at the Dockside because she needed to pick up a shift at the Grizzly Paw.

There would have been a time when my first response might have been to tell her to stuff it, but my half-sister was growing on me. We hadn't grown up together, and in reality, Ian and I spent most of the last ten years since discovering we even had two half-sisters ignoring their existence, as if it were our fault that our father was a lying, cheating asshole with two families. Being younger, and of similar ages, my younger brothers Cal and Declan had gotten to know both Chelsea and Amber, and it was Declan who'd bridged the gap earlier in the summer by sending Chelsea to live with Ian.

Things had a funny way of working out because after only a few weeks with her in my life, I couldn't imagine it any other way. Which was why I didn't hesitate, not really, when Chelsea asked for the favor. Even if it did mean eating my picnic food from a takeaway box she brought me on her break.

"You owe me." I opened the lid of the foam container. Immediately, the delicious aroma of fried chicken hit me. "This smells amazing."

"Only the best for you, bro. I made sure Jax put together a special box for you."

Jax was the head chef of the restaurant at the upscale Springs resort in town, and as far as I was concerned, cooked the best food I'd ever tasted.

"Okay." I picked up a drumstick. "Maybe you made up for it. This is amazing." I grabbed a beer out of the little fridge they kept in the store and headed outside, where I could listen to the music from the picnic.

Chelsea followed me out and together we sat on the edge of the dock and dangled our feet over the water's edge.

"Don't you have to get back?"

She shrugged. "Soon. It's actually pretty busy."

"I bet." I glanced in the direction of the party. "It looks like the whole town is there, but I know they're not, because there's at least a few people here renting boats and jet skis." I laughed and took another bite of the delicious chicken.

"I'm sorry you're missing it." Her pretty face fell into a frown. The last thing I wanted was for my little sister to be unhappy. My big brother instincts had kicked into overdrive in a big way. I had ten years to make up for, after all.

"Don't be sorry." I offered Chelsea a piece of chicken, but she shook her head. "I'm happy to help. Besides, it's good to see business booming. All business. If the Grizzly Paw is hopping, that's only good for the rest of the town, and Ian's going to be very happy when he sees the books from today.

We've been booked solid, and I even managed to book most of the slots for the next few days as well with walk-ins. The boats are going to be busy."

"That's so good." Chelsea's smile was back. "I know how hard Ian has worked to get things off the ground here."

"And you too."

She laughed. "My biggest contribution was being a pain in the ass, which resulted in Ian hiring Gwen to help out and we all know how that turned out." Her smile grew bigger and she kicked her legs excitedly. "Hey, want me to be a pain in your ass, too? Maybe that'll help you get a girlfriend."

I choked on the bite of potato salad in my mouth. I quickly washed it down with a slug of beer. "Girlfriend?" I managed to get the word out. "What would make you think I even wanted one?"

I was careful to keep my face a mask of neutrality because the truth was, I did kind of want one. It was a huge shift for me, one that even I was having trouble getting used to.

"I don't know if you do." Chelsea helped herself to a sip of beer. "But if you did, I think I have a real skill for this match-making by being a pain in the ass thing. If you're ever in need of my services…"

I laughed and snatched my beer back. "I'll keep it in mind."

The other thing I was keeping in mind was Jade. I'd barely seen her since the festival, but that didn't mean I hadn't been looking. At least a little. She may be the exact opposite of what I should be looking for—if I was indeed looking for a girlfriend—but damn, she was hot. And sexy as hell in bed. Or up against the wall, whatever the case may be.

"Well, don't say I didn't offer." Chelsea jumped to her feet and wiped her hands. "I meet a lot of nice women at the Paw. I'm sure I could—"

"I'm good, Chels." I held up a hand. "Really. I'll let you know if I need any help."

She pretended to pout for a minute before she squeezed me on the shoulder. "I should get back. But I'll see you later, right?"

"As soon as the last rental is back, which…judging by the sun, should be in about twenty minutes or so. I promise to find you and say hi." I was rewarded by her smile and once again, I was taken aback at how much time we'd missed growing up. I was five years older than her, and maybe it wouldn't have been the same when we were younger, but I was really enjoying having a little sister to look out for. And tease. There was no doubt that in only a few short weeks, Chelsea had her big brother completely wrapped around her little finger. But I didn't mind a bit.

"Okay, I'll see you soon. And thanks again." She turned to leave, but only got halfway down the dock before she turned around. "Oh, I totally forgot to tell you. I kind of volunteered you for something."

"Chelsea?" I drew out her name with a tone of warning. "Please tell me you didn't."

"You don't even know what it is. But you can't say no."

I was pretty sure I could say no. And I would, too, if it was anything ridiculous like being auctioned off in a bachelor auction. I had no reason to suspect that, but it seemed like something Chelsea would sign me up for.

"I swear, it's nothing bad." She took a few steps backward, closer to escape.

"Chels?"

"It's just some tutoring." I could see the mischief dancing in her eyes, even from the distance. "You're a teacher—she needs some help."

"She?" I dropped my head and shook it before I looked up again. "I told you I don't need a setup."

Her laughter floated on the breeze. "I didn't say anything about a setup. But if that's how you want to look at it... Besides, it's not for her; it's for her kid."

"Her kid?"

"I told you it wasn't a setup." She tipped her head playfully. "But now that you mention it."

"I didn't."

"Maybe you'd like——"

"Bye, Chelsea." There was zero point arguing with her, so I turned my attention back to the delicious food in front of me. At least that was something I could control, because I most certainly couldn't dream of controlling my sister.

I couldn't help but chuckle a little. But I still had no intention of letting Chelsea set me up with anyone. Although... My gaze drifted over the water toward the party that was starting to pick up steam as the band took the stage. If I planned on staying in Cedar Springs after the summer was over, it certainly couldn't hurt to meet new women. A vision of Jade's face flashed in my head.

Or maybe spend time with one I already knew.

No. It couldn't hurt at all.

JADE

I STOOD to the side of the party and gazed out over the lake. Not because I didn't know many people, and not because I wasn't really sure whether I fit into the various groups that had gathered along the lawn and next to the stage where the band was setting up. Although, both of those things were true. But avoiding a crowd was definitely not my style. No, I was leaning up against the large wooden sign on the sand declaring the welcome to Cedar Springs public beach because it gave me the best vantage point for another stunning sunset over the lake.

From the first night that I arrived in town, I'd been completely taken with the explosion of color that seemed to mark almost every sunset. The magnificent display of color was a kaleidoscope of yellows, purples, pinks, reds, and oranges. And the perfect calm of the water on a night like the one I was enjoying acted as a mirror to reflect a perfect replica of the beauty. It was truly one of the most beautiful things I'd ever seen.

"It's pretty spectacular, isn't it?"

My heart leapt at the sound of Mitch McCormick's voice. We'd seen each other a few times, but we certainly hadn't been alone together since…well, since he had my ass in his hands and my legs were wrapped around his waist. Heat flooded me at the thought.

Hoping I sounded a great deal more composed than I felt, I turned and smiled. "It is breathtaking."

"You're breathtaking."

My smile slipped a little. I had not been prepared for such direct flirting. Was he trying to secure a repeat performance of the festival? Or worse, a date?

No way. It wasn't happening.

"Thank you." I kept my voice cool and turned back to the scene in front of me. "Have you been enjoying the party?" Maybe a change of topic would give him the hint that I wasn't interested. And that was probably a good thing. Even if every cell in my body was vibrating for me to express to him exactly how interested I was.

"I am now."

Okay. Maybe he wasn't getting the hint.

I took a breath and prepared to tell him in no uncertain terms that despite the fact that we'd had a lot of fun together—and we had—it could never happen again.

"But truthfully, I just got here," Mitch continued. "I've been so busy helping Ian with the Dockside for the last few weeks, it shouldn't surprise me that it cut into party time, too. But I'm here now." He glanced down at my empty hands. "You need a drink." It wasn't a question.

By self-imposed rule, I usually limited myself to two glasses of wine. Three, if I was at a longer event and then I'd only drink spritzers. Less alcohol that way. My mother had drilled it into my head that drinking too much alcohol only led to one thing—poor choices.

But I'd been completely sober the night of the summer solstice festival. I looked over at Mitch, who looked even sexier in his cargo shorts and T-shirt than he had the night of the festival. And that hadn't been such a poor choice.

"I'd love a drink." My smile was genuine as I turned with Mitch and walked with him toward the bar. We didn't touch, but the heat coming from him warmed me from the slight chill in the air now that the sun had gone down.

"Two big events in less than a month," Mitch said as we approached the crowd. "You're really fitting in to this small-town life, aren't you?"

"I don't know about fitting in." I straightened my shoulders, suddenly hyper aware of the silk blouse I wore tucked neatly into black dress shorts. If I was trying to fit in, I definitely wasn't pulling it off with my outfit. All the women around me were wearing cutoff shorts, cut tank tops or flirty summer dresses. I looked more like I was ready to attend a conference or a business meeting of some sort. Which was ironic, considering I'd changed into something more casual after my meeting with Gwen and Ian, which was casual. "I could say the same about you." I shifted the conversation back to him. "You are a city boy after all, aren't you?"

The sexy smile slid from his face, but only momentarily. "Guilty. But I can play at being a townie, can't I?"

"If you can, I can."

I was flirting. With Mitch, it was either that or we were snapping at each other. In fact, it was that initial heat between us that had sparked things with us from the beginning. It was a heat that was still most definitely there. But I shouldn't encourage it. Fooling around once was one thing. But twice? That bordered way too closely to a relationship of some kind.

"What does that mean?" he asked.

We approached the makeshift bar set up outside the Grizzly Paw. Mitch waved to the bartender, who was tending customers at the other end. He held up two fingers and turned his attention back to me.

"You're enjoying Cedar Springs then?"

"Well, I wouldn't say I'm not enjoying it."

Mitch shook his head and chuckled. "I'm not entirely sure what that means."

"There are definitely perks." I could have died. Did I seriously just say that? So much for not flirting. No good could come from leading Mitch on. At least, no long-term good. The short-term good would be very good indeed. But I needed to focus. Especially if I intended on sticking around past the summer. "That's not what I meant," I said quickly. "I was just saying that working and living so close is really handy."

Mitch gave me a strange look. "Somehow, I don't think that's what you were saying. At least I hope that it wasn't."

"No." I put my hand on his arm, way more flustered than I ever liked to be. I could not have Mitch thinking that I was the type of woman who—what? What type of woman was I? I wasn't the type who had relationships. That was for damn sure. And before Mitch, the last man I'd slept with had been a friend of a colleague who'd attended some random work function. And that was so many years ago, I could barely remember it. No. The only relationship I had was with my vibrator. It was sad, but all too true.

Not that I could stand there surrounded by people and explain that to him. Especially considering the bartender chose that moment to reach across the bar and hand Mitch two beers. "Chelsea said to put it on her tab," the man said. "Have a good night."

Mitch nodded his thanks and handed me one of the bottles. "Cheers."

"Beer?"

"Sorry. I should have asked. You do drink beer, don't you?"

"Beer's fine. Thanks." I didn't, but for whatever reason, that didn't seem important. I put the bottle to my lips and tasted the slightly sour liquid. I couldn't remember the last time I'd had a beer, but it wasn't that bad. Perfect for a summer night. My mother really wouldn't approve. I took a deeper sip before Mitch led us back through the crowd, to an empty picnic table.

"So, you were telling me that this town had a few perks." He winked and slid his hand across to mine.

His touch sent heat racing through me, directly between my legs, where it pooled instantly because I knew exactly how, if we were alone, that touch could make me feel. Good. Damn good. And despite the fact that we had barely said two words to each other for the last few weeks, it was clear that Mitch felt the same way. It would be so easy to let myself fall into his arms again. After all, what would one more night hurt?

Men are nothing but trouble, Jade. They'll ruin everything you've worked so hard for. I could practically hear my mother's voice next to me. I jerked my hand away and drank deeply from my bottle.

"About the other night," I said before I could stop myself.

"Right." Mitch rolled his own bottle between his hands. "The other night was—"

"A mistake."

"A mistake?" He sat back and didn't even try to hide the shock on his face. "Somehow, I didn't expect you to say that."

Shit. I was screwing this up.

"It wasn't a mistake so much as…"

"As a what?" Mitch crossed his arms. His biceps bulged in a deliciously distracting way.

I swallowed hard. "It was a…it was…well, it just shouldn't have happened, is all. I don't usually do that kind of thing, and I'm sure you're used to—"

"Whoa." Mitch held up a hand to stop me. "I'm not sure what you're trying to say, but I'm not 'used to' anything. I'm sorry if you think the other night shouldn't have happened. But I really enjoyed myself. So I can't say the same."

That was it. I wanted to completely self-combust. I was making an ass out of myself, and the last thing I wanted was for Mitch to think I hadn't enjoyed myself. I had. A lot. Too much. But that wasn't the point either.

"I'm not saying I didn't."

"So you did?"

I took a deep breath, smoothed my hair back and tried again. I was the queen of composure. I'd worked for years on perfecting exactly the right way to present myself to the world and I wasn't about to let Mitch McCormick ruin that with that sexy, sly smile of his. Internally, I counted to ten. "What I'm saying is that the other night was fine."

"Fine?"

I ignored him. "But there can never be anything more between us. I'm a business woman and my career comes first."

"Before fun?"

"I didn't say that."

"But you did imply it."

I kept my mouth pressed into a line and stared him directly in his eyes. His deep, sexy eyes. "That's not what I was—"

"Career and fun," he interrupted me. "The two things do not have to be mutually exclusive, you know?"

"I know that." Did I? "I was just trying to—"

"Mitch!" A voice interrupted us, and we both looked behind us to where Mitch's little sister, Chelsea, stood with a tray. She waved at him enthusiastically when she saw she had his attention. "Come over here. I need you to meet someone."

Mitch raised his beer in recognition before he turned back to me. "Excuse me for a moment. I'll be back." He stood from the table. "But just for the record, if you're trying to tell me you're not looking for anything serious, don't worry."

I sat back, shocked. "Don't worry?"

"Yeah." He winked at me. "You're not really my type."

MITCH

I'D BEEN A TOTAL ASSHOLE.

Not my type? Of course she was my type: hot, sexy, strong, confident woman who was an absolute wildcat in bed. Jade Johnson was nothing but my type.

The problem was, I wasn't hers. That much was clear. She'd avoided me since we hooked up, barely looked me in the eyes when we had found ourselves in the same room together, and now she was telling me we'd been a mistake...a mistake?

Nothing about the sex between us had been a mistake. That much I was certain of.

I didn't have time to think about it at the moment anyway. Chelsea stood at the bar. I had a feeling she was ready to make an introduction and attempt a setup. And maybe that wouldn't be so bad anyway. Jade Johnson was obviously not the right type of woman for me. A woman like Jade, who put career before all else, would only mean trouble. Besides, I'd already decided that a high-maintenance city girl was most definitely not my type. Maybe I hadn't been lying after all. And really, I'd had more than enough drama with Bethany. I was not in a hurry for any more. No. I needed a good, drama-free girl who I could try to build a life with. A future.

And maybe that future could be in Cedar Springs. Ian was right; getting away from the city this summer and being at the lake was good for the soul. And I'd only been there less than a month. Imagine what the rest of the summer could do for my well-being? Let alone a lifetime in the mountains.

It was definitely something I wanted to imagine. The more I thought about it, the more it felt right.

Really right.

"Mitch." Chelsea's voice jarred me out of my imagination. I put a smile on my face, even though my little sister had that look on her pretty face that told me I was in trouble. Like the kind of trouble that meant a setup. "Come on." She waved her hand. "Get over here. There's someone I want you to meet."

"Chels…" My voice held a warning, but if she heard it, she ignored it.

"You could have dressed up," she hissed in my ear. "It's a party for God's sake, Mitch."

"It's a picnic." I corrected her and like the good brother I was, walked with her toward the woman standing off to the side. The woman I was more and more sure I was about to be set up with. "And I look fine because you're not going to set me up with anyone tonight, right, Chels?"

She ignored me again. "Remember when I told you earlier that I had a friend who needed tutoring?"

I had to work hard to keep from rolling my eyes. "You said her kid needed tutoring."

"Same difference." We stopped next to a very pretty, very sweet, very nice woman.

Maybe a setup wouldn't be so bad after all. Clearly,

Chelsea knew me better than I knew myself. Or at least, she had good-looking friends.

"Evelyn, I want you to meet my brother, Mitch." Chelsea presented me with a flourish of her hand, as if she were working on a game show. "Mitch, this is Evelyn Rose."

"Evie, please." She held out her hand with a shy smile.

Definitely a nice girl.

Perfect.

"It's nice to meet you, Evie." I flashed her my most devastating smile. "Any friend of Chelsea's is a—"

"Well, I don't really know Chelsea all that well." Evie blushed and ducked her head. She was shy. The exact opposite of Jade.

Where had that thought come from?

I was just introduced to a beautiful woman who was much more in line with the type of woman I should be dating. Why the hell had thoughts of Jade popped in my head? I had to force myself not to look in the direction where I knew Jade was sitting. Was she watching me meet this woman? Was she jealous? Why did I care?

I forced myself to focus on the pretty woman in front of me. "Well, it's nice to meet you. Happy Canada Day."

"To you as well." When she smiled, she was even prettier. "Chelsea said you might be able to help me out."

Right. Tutoring. Here I was thinking about dating the woman and all she was looking for was a tutor. I really needed to get over myself and stop having such a one-track mind.

"I can try. I usually teach middle school. What kind of classes are you taking?"

Evie's laugh filled the space between us. "Oh, no. It's not for me." Her arm reached out and her hand landed briefly on my forearm before it fluttered away. "It's my son."

"Your son?" I tried not to sound surprised, but I was sure I totally failed because I was surprised. This woman barely looked old enough to have a child at all, let alone a son who required tutoring.

"I told you that, remember?" Chelsea smiled knowingly. "He doesn't listen to me," she said to Evie.

"I'm sorry," I said genuinely. "I just didn't…well…honestly, you look much too young to have a school-aged child."

A shadow darkened her face, but only for a moment before she smiled again. "Thank you. I can hardly believe it myself some days. But Jonah is eight already and really struggling with math. I know he's a little younger than you're used to teaching, but I really think a different teaching style might help. He tried so hard last year and just could not wrap his head around it all."

"I'm willing to give it a try."

I was? When Chelsea had mentioned the idea of tutoring, my initial reaction had been hell no. I'd wanted nothing more than a break from my teaching job in the city. A break from curriculums, from students, demanding faculty, and meddling parents. I needed a break from everything.

Or maybe it had been a break from my life in general I'd been looking for?

Whatever it was, I'd been enjoying it since coming to Cedar Springs. Spending the summer working at the marina. Driving boats, playing on jet skis, swimming in the lake, and flirting with women were all part of the plan.

Teaching a troubled kid was not.

"You're probably right," I continued, unsure of how the words were coming out of my mouth. "He probably just needs a different teaching approach."

"And Mitch is the best." Chelsea put her arm around my waist and squeezed.

"Thank you so much." Evie reached into her purse and pulled out a piece of paper that she pressed into my hand. "This is my cell phone number. I know you're probably really busy so I'm totally willing to work around your schedule and of course I'll pay you. I just am so grateful that Jonah can get a leg up this summer. It would just be devastating if he had to repeat a grade. I mean—"

"Not to worry." I smiled reassuringly. "He'll be fine."

Evie threw her arms around me in a spontaneous hug. She smelled like strawberries and sugar. Almost exactly what I'd expect her to smell like. I breathed her in. It was nice and for the briefest moment, I closed my eyes. But then the hug was over and my eyes opened and I was staring across the lawn, directly at Jade. Who, judging by the way she stared back at me before she slammed her beer bottle on the table, had also seen the hug.

Chapter Three

JADE

IT WAS STUPID.

No. It was ridiculous.

But it didn't matter how I reasoned it—I was pissed. It was bad enough he'd left me sitting there alone, but to flirt with another woman right in front of me? That was just rude.

Even if I didn't want anything more to do with him in that way, it was still rude.

I tried to take a deep breath and calm my breathing. But it didn't work, which just upset me more.

I never got worked up over a man. I never let myself get close enough to anyone to even have the chance. And of all men, Mitch? He'd literally, only moments earlier, told me to my face that I wasn't his type. That should have been enough to stem any flow of feelings I might think I was having.

But it wasn't.

Dammit.

He was walking toward me.

The last thing I needed was to hear about how he'd just

made a date with the perfectly pretty woman who probably made pies for charity bake sales and volunteered at the hospital, cuddling babies. I unwound my legs as gracefully as I could from the picnic table and moved quickly across the great lawn, toward the lake. Away from Mitch.

"Hey. Wait up."

I kept walking.

"Jade."

I straightened my shoulders.

"Seriously." A hand grabbed me and jerked me back. "Slow down," Mitch said, when he was already looking me in the eyes.

"Let go of me," I hissed and shook off his touch.

Mitch held both hands in front of him in surrender. "Sorry. I didn't mean to upset you. I was just trying to catch you before you left." He tilted his head and examined me with thought. "Why were you leaving? I thought we were having a drink together."

"We did." I worked hard to keep the emotion out of my voice. I did not want him thinking I was jealous or felt slighted or really, that I was feeling any other emotion besides indifference toward him. "We were done. It was time to go."

"I don't think it's time at all. The fireworks haven't even started."

"Fireworks?" I half expected him to make a smart ass comment about the fireworks between us. But it was obviously just me who was thinking that way. And those thoughts were about to change, just as soon as I got away from him and could think clearly. There was something about being near Mitch that clouded my thoughts.

I needed space.

"Yes," he said. "You have to see the fireworks. Cedar Springs puts on a show that would rival any major city. They're amazing."

"Really?"

Was I seriously considering staying? With Mitch?

He shrugged. "They used to anyway. I've been really looking forward to seeing if they live up to my memories. Stay."

I glanced back toward the bar, but the woman he'd been flirting with a moment ago was gone. "Won't your girlfriend mind?"

What had possessed me to say that? I really was losing it. I was just not that type of woman. I didn't care about things like that. I didn't get attached to men and I most certainly was not jealous.

The corner of Mitch's lips ticked up. "My girlfriend?"

I waved in the direction of the bar. "The woman...you were talking...I saw her...never mind." I turned to walk away again, but Mitch quickly stepped in front of me.

"Oh, no. I think I want to hear more."

His grin was a full-fledged smile now. Curse him if it wasn't the sexiest smile I'd ever seen.

"Were you jealous that I was talking to Evelyn?"

"Evelyn? That's her name?" I shook my head hard and wouldn't meet his gaze.

"That's her name. You were jealous."

"No." I wasn't. Was I?

"You were." He took my hand. "It's okay."

I pulled my hand away. It was most certainly not okay. I wasn't a jealous person. I didn't get jealous over anything or anyone. Let alone a man. This was ridiculous. Spending time with Mitch was ridiculous. It needed to come to an end. Now.

"I should go."

"Don't." His voice was soft, the teasing tone gone. I turned to look at him. "I won't tease you." He sounded genuine. "But I really don't want you to miss the fireworks."

I considered it. Seriously. I didn't want to miss the fireworks either. But that wasn't the real reason I didn't want to leave. It was Mitch. God help me, I liked spending time with him. Whether it was a good idea or not.

"Please."

He raised his eyebrows, making him look way more innocent than I knew he actually was. But it worked. I nodded.

"Okay. I'll stay."

Mitch's face immediately split into a smile. "Wait right here." Before I could object, he ran toward the bar. I watched as he handed the bartender some money and a few minutes later, he walked across the lawn toward me with a bag in his hand and a satisfied grin on his face.

"Ready?" Before I could answer, he grabbed my hand and started jogging with me in tow.

I found myself smiling and laughing and even squealing a little bit like a schoolgirl. "Slow down." I risked a glance down at my strappy leather sandals, which looked killer with my outfit, but were definitely not the most practical footwear for a jog across the lawn. "My shoes are—" As if to save myself from any further explanation, my toe caught on a rock and my body propelled forward. "Ouch!"

My hurt would have been far greater, if Mitch hadn't been holding my hand. His instincts were on point and he easily pulled me up and wrapped his arm around me, holding me briefly against his chest before he released me.

"Are you okay?"

For a moment, the entire world was on mute. Everything ceased to exist except for how damned good he smelled, how warm he was, and how amazing his arm felt around me. And then in a whoosh of sound, I regained my senses. "I'm fine." I managed to get the words out right before the searing pain in my foot took over and I looked down. "Oh my God. My toe!"

"Whoa. You really banged it."

I was well aware of that because I was currently jumping

around like a complete fool because of the hot pain in my big toe.

"Come here. It's okay."

I was vaguely aware of Mitch trying to soothe me. That was until he scooped me up in his arms as if I were a small child.

"Mitch, I'm fine," I objected.

"Right." He raised an eyebrow in question. "I can see that."

I didn't object further because my toe did hurt. A lot. More than I could have imagined for such a small appendage. Besides that, it felt good to be pressed up against his chest. Dammed good. And I may be a hot mess when it came to knowing how I felt about Mitch, but at that very moment, there was no other place I'd rather be.

MITCH

SHE WAS SO LIGHT. But despite her slight body, she felt absolutely perfect in my arms. She fit. My dick twitched in response to her proximity, agreeing with my assessment.

But I couldn't focus on whatever it was I was feeling for Jade. She was hurt, and that had to be my first priority.

Getting her naked would come later.

That thought hit me out of the blue. Well, not entirely out of the blue. But still, not only ten minutes ago I'd been determined not to get involved with a woman like Jade. Not that it mattered. I only had to spend a few minutes sparring with her, feeling the sting of her tongue, the heat of her eyes upon me, inhaling the sexy spice that was her scent, and I wanted her. Bad.

"Mitch. Seriously. I can walk."

"Maybe so." I forced myself to be serious. "But I think we should use precautions until we know what we're dealing with."

She laughed, and the sound went right to the core of me. "We're dealing with a stubbed toe and a bruised ego. I feel stupid."

I squeezed her tighter to my chest and continued to walk across the great lawn, away from the party and toward the marina. "It's not stupid. You're injured. I have a first-aid kit at the Dockside. I'll take a look."

She argued with me for the duration of the walk, but she didn't try to get out of my arms. If anything, she snuggled in closer. I liked it.

I finally set her gingerly on her feet outside of the Dockside. "Give me a second and I'll unlock the door and turn some lights on. Don't put weight on it."

Even in the dim light, I was pretty sure I could see her rolling her eyes. "It's not broken, Mitch. I'm fine. I promise."

I unlocked the door, put the bag I was still carrying on the counter and flicked on the light before I went back to where I left her. I was fully prepared to scoop her up in my arms again, but the look on her face warned me to back off a little. Begrudgingly, I did so, opting to put an arm around her shoulder to help her hop over to a chair. I fetched the first-aid kit and rolled another chair across from where Jade sat. "Let me see."

She lifted her slender leg and I slid my hands down her soft skin, from her knee to her ankle, until she rested her foot on my knee. I could have happily spent the rest of the night running my hands up and down that sexy leg, but the damage to her toe demanded attention. "Oh, that doesn't look good." Her big toe had a nasty gash along the top fleshy part of it. Bits of dirt and grass clung to the bloody area. "We should get it cleaned up. Can you move it?"

She flexed her foot and flinched.

"Maybe don't try to move it for now. It's probably not broken, but more likely it's badly sprained. Best to let it rest." I slipped her shoe off and dropped it next to the chair. "Pretty shoes."

"Not very practical, I guess." She shrugged. "But I've never been to a small-town Canada Day party. Not that I've been to many Canada Day parties at all. But still, maybe I should get some new footwear."

Without moving her foot from my lap, I cleaned up her toe with the supplies from the kit. "I thought you looked nice. Your shoes are sexy."

"Sexy?" She laughed. "I can't imagine it's very sexy to be cleaning my bloody toe."

"Actually." I paused and looked up. When she met my eyes, I said, "Everything about you is sexy."

She didn't say anything right away, but she didn't look away. I took that as a win. I was the first to look away, but only because I needed to get the gauze from the kit.

"I don't think you should get rid of the shoes," I said. "But maybe some flip-flops might be a good addition for lake life, don't you think?" I wound the gauze around her toe.

"Honestly?" I nodded and she continued. "I have no idea what's appropriate for lake life. I've never spent any time at a lake."

"Never?"

She shook her head. "My mom was pretty strict and she hated anything that had to do with the outdoors. It was a big deal to get her to take me to the park." She smiled, clearly trying to make light of the situation, but I was appalled. I quickly finished wrapping her toe, tucking the edges in to finish the job.

"I think that's terrible," I declared. "But I also think that my plan for tonight will be that much better. If you're up for it?" I gestured to her toe.

Jade laughed and pulled her leg away, preparing to stand. "I told you. It's just a—ouch!" She plopped back into the chair when standing didn't work out the way she'd hoped. "Okay, it hurts. But I still want to see the fireworks. You promised they were awesome."

"And they are." I stood, grabbed the bag I'd left on the counter and a set of keys from the wall before once more scooping her up into my arms. "Let me show you."

JADE

I PROBABLY SHOULDN'T LIKE it so much, but I couldn't help it. I liked being in his arms. And for the moment, I didn't care because something about the way he naturally took care of me made me feel more special than I'd ever felt before. And even if nothing ever happened between us again, I still enjoyed it. As far as I could tell, there was nothing wrong with that.

For a woman who always needed to be in control, it surprised me that I was so willing to let Mitch take charge. But there was something about the way he handled me—it was nice to let go once in a while.

"Where are we going?" I twisted my head around so I could see where he was taking me and it didn't require an answer. Mitch walked across and down the docks, toward the boats that were tied up for the night. He stopped next to one particularly nice boat and set me down.

"We're not seriously...I mean you can't be...a boat? Now?"

"Of course a boat." He hopped off the dock, into the boat

in question, and tucked the bag he was carrying away under the seat before he reached out a hand to me. "Come on in."

A boat? There was no way. I'd never been on a boat, let alone at night. Was it safe? What if something went wrong? I didn't know the first thing about a boat. Hell, I couldn't remember the last time I'd even been swimming.

I shook my head and tried to take a step backward until I was most unceremoniously reminded of the pain in my toe. *Dammit.*

"What's wrong?" Mitch grinned as soon as he realized what the problem was. "You're afraid of boats."

I shook my head.

"You are." He stepped back onto the dock and took a step toward me.

"I am not." I straightened my shoulders and tried to look braver than I felt. The truth was the boat terrified me because I was scared of the unknown.

Mitch slid his hand down my bare arm and squeezed gently. "You don't have to be afraid. I'm here." He took a step forward and I let him lead me. "I grew up on boats. There's nothing safer and more fun. Besides, you're with a man who definitely knows what he's doing."

His words sparked all kinds of innuendo but I was too busy focusing on the machine floating in the water to react.

"You got this, Jade." He lifted me by the waist and before I realized what he was doing, he placed me gently inside the boat. "Sit right there. I promise I'll take care of you."

I didn't argue, partly because I knew I was being ridiculous but mostly because I was curious.

Besides, I had nothing better to do and I really did want to see the fireworks. The fact that I could see them with Mitch by my side was only a bonus.

"Are you going to be okay?" he questioned. "Because I really think you're going to like this."

I nodded. Not only would I be okay—I would be more than okay. And maybe nothing was going to happen with Mitch, but at least for the night I could allow myself to enjoy the fireworks and the company of a sexy man. He didn't have to be anything more.

I ignored the little voice in my head that told me I was a liar, because I knew it. Just being next to Mitch was something.

"You look like you're thinking about something."

I shook my head again. "No," I said. "Well, that's not entirely true. I'm thinking that you're right, this will be fine. I'm actually excited." My laugh bubbled up from deep inside me. "And I think it's more than a little ridiculous that I'm a grown woman who has never been on a boat in a lake."

Mitch turned the key and the engine fired up with a low rumble. I had expected it to sound more like a car. I didn't know why. But it had a unique sound and a feel beneath me.

He leaned over to untie the rope that held the backend of the boat. "I wasn't going to say anything," he said. "But it does seem a little crazy that you've never been in a boat. But honestly?" He looked me straight in the eye and a thrill went through my body. "I'm really glad that I'm the man who gets to show you this."

Mitch moved to the front of the boat into the driver's seat. He leaned over briefly to untie the last line that connected us to the dock before he put his hands on the wheel. He put the boat into gear and slowly started to move away from the dock into the black night.

"It's so dark out here." I glanced around, not sure what I should expect. I knew that it wasn't like a road, where there were other cars or other boats. Maybe I expected something like a light of some kind, but as the marina faded in the distance there really was nothing but black expanse in front of us, the stars overhead, and the moon glowing and reflecting off the lake.

It was both beautiful and kind of spooky at the same time, but despite that, I in no way felt unsafe.

"I wanted to wait until we got away from the dock to turn on the lights," Mitch said. "But look." He flicked a switch on the dashboard and at once the boat was illuminated in the soft glow, and we could see a little farther ahead of us in the water. "See? We're perfectly safe out here." There was a teasing tone in his voice, but I ignored it. "And really? There's nothing for us to hit out here."

"Are there other boats?"

"Sometimes, yes. But it's a big lake, and most of the time when I take the boat out at night, I have the place to myself. It's kind of like my own private lake." He looked out over the steering wheel into the darkness and for a moment I felt as if I were intruding on a private moment.

I was quiet for a moment, as he was clearly lost in a memory. But then the moment was over, and Mitch looked at me with a smile. "Are you ready for this?"

I knew what he was asking and, surprisingly, I was ready. "I am."

Mitch grinned and didn't need to ask twice. He pushed down on the throttle and the boat moved forward in the smooth motion of a fine machine. It picked up speed so quickly, slicing across the flat, dark water, that for a moment I forgot that I'd been nervous at all. And when Mitch threw back his head and laughed up at the moon, I found myself doing the same thing.

Never before in my life had I laughed at the moon or howled out loud the way I just had. For some reason, that idea struck me funny and I did it again and again and again.

I sat up straight, shook out my hair and let the wind blow the strands behind me. The cool night air tickled my face as the boat continued to fly across the surface.

Next to me, Mitch was laughing and shouting right along

with me. Like two teenagers who had been given the first freedom they'd ever experienced. We howled through the night air until finally Mitch eased up on the throttle and the boat slowed.

I sat back in the chair and to my surprise found tears streaking down my face.

Mitch looked over at me. "It's the wind," he said. "It can sting your eyes, make you tear up and you don't even notice. Are you okay? I didn't go too fast, did I? For your first time, I mean."

I looked at him. He had such a serious look on his face, totally oblivious of the fact that he just said the most suggestive thing he could have to me. I couldn't help myself; I burst out laughing.

Everything about the night had been ridiculous: from being jealous of him talking to another woman, to stubbing my toe, to howling at the moon, to racing across the lake in a boat.

The other woman.

No. That hadn't been ridiculous; I had been jealous. Not that I was about to let him know that. After all, he'd made it very clear I wasn't his type. And that was okay because he wasn't mine either. I needed to remember that we were just friends.

"I'm fine." I laughed. "My first time was awesome. In fact, I loved it. I can see why you enjoy it so much. It's absolutely exhilarating."

I used my fingers to brush out my hair as Mitch turned off the engine and we floated in the middle of the lake. I tipped my head back and looked up to the night sky, where the stars were starting to form. I'd never seen so many stars living in the city. Hell, I was lucky to see any at all.

"It's beautiful out here."

"You're beautiful."

I sat up and looked across the boat to Mitch.

"I shouldn't have—"

"What did you—"

We spoke at the same time.

Mitch shook his head. "I'm sorry," he said. "You go first."

"What did you mean before when you said I wasn't your type?"

The second the question was out of my mouth, I wanted to take it back. I didn't want to know why I wasn't his type.

"I shouldn't have said that." He shook his head. "It's not that you're not my type," he said with a small smile. "Because clearly you are. I think we can both agree that we had a lot of fun together."

"It's okay," I said with a small laugh. "We did have fun together. And it's okay if I'm not really your type because like I said earlier, I'm not interested in you like that. But that's okay, because friends don't need a type, right?"

"So we're friends now?"

"We are, don't you think?"

Mitch nodded. "I'd like that. I'd like that a lot."

MITCH

I WAS A LYING BASTARD. Because I wasn't going to like that; I wasn't going to like just being friends with Jade at all. At least that was what my body was telling me.

The way my dick twitched in my pants whenever she was close told me that what I really wanted was to be more than friends—a lot more. But my dick wasn't my brain, and even if this woman wasn't the right kind of woman for me, that didn't change how it felt.

And she was holding me at arm's length, the same way I

was doing with her. Just being friends was definitely the best option, for both of us.

"How's your toe?" I moved away from the steering wheel, toward the back of the boat and the big bench seat. I lifted up the cushion, pulled out a blanket that I kept there, and spread it out along the vinyl. "This is the best place to watch the fireworks. And I did promise you that the fireworks show in Cedar Springs was legendary, didn't I?"

She laughed. "Yes, you did. And I really hope they live up to the hype, or I'm going to have to question my new friend's judgment."

"Don't worry, don't worry. You're going to love it."

I took the beers out of the bag and put them down next to me before I reached my hand out to Jade. "You'll want to come sit back here. It's more comfortable. And it's way better to watch from."

Not to mention the fact that I wanted to be close to her. I couldn't help that even though I knew I shouldn't want to be, I did. Something about her energy called to me and pulled me to her.

She took my hand and, on one foot, hopped to the back of the boat to sit next to me.

Damn, she smelled good. Spicy with just a touch of sweet. She actually reminded me of the bakery, Dream Puffs, on Main Street and the cinnamon buns Suzy was famous for.

What was wrong with me?

Now I was comparing her to baking? It was ridiculous. I was ridiculous. But I couldn't seem to stop myself, just the same way I couldn't stop myself from wanting to touch her.

But I wouldn't.

Not unless she wanted me to.

Friends.

It was going to be difficult because every time I looked at her, I wanted to rip her clothes off, slide my hands down her body and kiss her until she begged me to be inside her. I didn't know what kind of friendship that was, but damned if I didn't want to find out.

"What are you thinking about?"

I shook my head in a futile effort to pull myself together. There was no way I was going to tell her, especially if we wanted this friendship thing to work.

"Can I get you a beer?" It was better to change the subject altogether.

She shook her head and then shrugged. "I don't usually drink beer," she said. "In fact, I can't remember the last time I had one."

"Oh." Disappointment flashed through me. I wanted to please her in the craziest way. "I wish I had known that. I would've got something else. You know what? I should have known."

She tilted her head and eyed me. "Why should you have known that?"

"You don't really seem like a beer type of woman." She really didn't. But judging by the way her face transformed, she was definitely going to take that as a challenge. Something else that didn't surprise me.

"I can be a beer type of woman if I want," she said with the sassiest edge of defiance. "Besides, I kind of like it." She took the beer from my hand and took a little sip.

I pretended not to notice the little grimace she made when the liquid hit her lips. It was cute, and not a lot about Jade was cute. She was too damn sexy to be cute.

"Well, I'm glad you're open to it," I said. "Because fireworks just aren't the same without a drink. And I'll be honest with you, the best way to watch fireworks in the middle of the lake is with a cold beer."

She laughed. "It sure sounds like you're an expert at fireworks watching."

"I haven't done this in years," I admitted. "But it used to be one of my favorite parts of summer." In truth, I had been looking forward to Canada Day from the moment I got back to town, for this very reason. When I was a kid, going out in the boat to watch the fireworks was almost a rite of passage. Our mom would only let us go when we were old enough to be responsible. For me, that meant thirteen but only because Ian was fifteen and responsible enough for both of us.

I could still remember that night when Mom had given us permission. We'd felt so grown up, like such big men full of the responsibility, when in reality we'd been so nervous that we were going to get lost or lose our way that we didn't even go all the way down the lake toward town where the fireworks viewing would be the best. We stayed close to our home dock and only caught glimpses of the highest explosions.

But it meant that we got back safely, Mom had been happy, and we still went to bed that night thrilled with the responsibility we'd been given. In the years following, taking the boat out on the water for Canada Day became more of a group event with our friends from town and a few girls.

Oh, the girls.

I always had a girlfriend for the summer and taking them out on the boat with me, sitting on the back just the way I was doing with Jade right now—with my arm around their shoulders in the dark as the bright lights burst overhead—always guaranteed me a kiss. I wasn't expecting a kiss from Jade tonight, not that it wouldn't be welcome. But I was determined to behave. I wasn't a teenager anymore; I could control myself. I could make the right decision. And dammit, I would prove that to myself.

"So what do you think about your first boat experience?" I took a sip of my own beer and watched her face light up with a smile. "I know it's kind of strange for your first time to be at night, and we will have to correct that with a ride in the

44

daylight. I promise it will be very different. But just as awesome."

"It's fantastic," she said. "Thank you." She stared at me for a minute, as if she was going to say something else. But right then, the first firecracker shot into the air with a streak of red and burst into a bright explosion overhead. Jade squealed and grabbed my hand.

"It's starting. Look up." We tilted our heads back together as the light show began in earnest. Green, blue, yellow, orange, red. The explosions came one after another, lighting up the night sky and obliterating the stars for their colorful show. Next to me, Jade was oohing and ahhing, totally lost in the show overhead.

"Mitch, this is awesome." Her face was lit up with color, but it was her smile that mesmerized me. "It's like we have our own private show." She looked back up to the sky, the smile in her face only getting bigger.

For a woman as mature and sophisticated as Jade was, something about her was still so innocent, as though she hadn't experienced life. And in that moment, I knew—friends or lovers—I wanted to show her things. I wanted to show her life.

The fireworks show was forgotten as I watched her instead. At one point, my hand slid across the seat and covered hers but she didn't shake it off. In fact, she turned it over and wrapped her fingers around mine. It sent a thrill through my body. And it might've just been the fireworks, or the dark, or the beers, but it didn't matter. The moment was right and before I could talk myself out of it, or remind myself we were only supposed to be friends, I leaned over, slid one hand behind her head and pulled her to my lips.

I expected her to push me away; after all, we'd made such a big deal about only wanting to be friends. But the second our lips touched, the heat I remembered from the summer solstice festival was back. She made a small groaning sound, and just like that, I was lost. My other hand left hers to wrap around her body and pulled her closer to me. Jade was just as hungry for my touch as I was for hers. Her hands slid down my back, leaving trails of heat and fire behind them.

The fireworks continued to blast overhead, illuminating our passion.

"I know we're friends."

Jade nodded. "Friends," she agreed. "But maybe…just for tonight…"

"Tonight we can be really good friends. I mean, just for tonight." I dropped my mouth to her neck and sucked just below her earlobe. A move that elicited a shiver and another groan. "Because sometimes friends are really close." I knew I was talking shit, but the effort to justify what we were doing and what we were about to do seemed important.

"I agree." She let out a moan as I went back to kissing her neck.

I liked to make her moan. It was one of the sexiest sounds I'd ever heard.

There were too many clothes between us. Pulling away just far enough to rip my T-shirt off and toss it in the bottom of the boat, I turned my attention to her blouse, tugging at her buttons.

"Easy, easy." She laughed and took control of sliding the buttons out. With her blouse open, her breasts clothed only in a lacy white bra and her pink nipples standing at attention, I thought it might be the undoing of me altogether.

"You are so damn sexy." With both my hands, I slipped her blouse off her shoulders and tossed it to the bottom of the boat with my T-shirt. And because I couldn't wait one more second, I pulled her close and nestled my face between her breasts, inhaling the intoxicating scent of her—letting it fill me, letting it fuel me. I turned my attention to one breast, sucking her nipples into my mouth through the lacy fabric. She groaned and arched her back, encouraging me. With my free hand, I flicked my thumb over her other nipple while my tongue worked, sucked, and pulled more moans from within her.

Fireworks continued to pop and bang above us, but neither of us had any attention to spare.

"Mitch, I need you."

I didn't have to be asked twice. I needed her just as badly. Reluctantly, I left her breasts and sat up to pull her back on the bench just far enough to lay her down comfortably. Aware of her sore foot, I slipped her shorts gingerly over her legs and discarded them with the rest of the clothing before I shucked my own shorts.

I knelt between her legs and let my hands travel up the inside of her smooth, long legs. I briefly teased her with my fingers, but the need growing between us was only getting stronger. She reached out to find my dick, hard and at attention.

The touch of her on my skin made me crazy. "Damn, woman. You are… Just… Damn."

"The feeling is more than mutual. Now get down here."

"You're so damn bossy." I grinned, but we both knew I wasn't going to disobey. She liked to be in charge, that was clear. Not that I didn't like it, but my mind ran wild with thoughts of what it would be like to have her beneath me, totally at my mercy, to tease, to please, to make scream. Yes, I couldn't think of anything hotter than showing her who could really be in control.

But the reality in front of me was pretty fucking sexy, too.

"I know what I want," she breathed. Her breasts heaved, straining at the lace of her bra. "And I want *you*, now."

I moved until I was over her, my cock poised at her entrance. Supporting myself on one hand, I reached up and pulled the lace of her bra down, under each breast, exposing them to the night air…and my eyes. Beneath me, Jade wiggled and pressed her hips up to meet me. With one thrust, I was inside her. She was so hot, so tight, so perfect.

"Yes. You feel so good." Jade tipped her head back, her eyes open and looking into mine.

I knew I wasn't going to last long. But it didn't matter, because I knew we would both come together. Jade's hand clenched my ass; her fingers dug into my flesh as I moved inside her. Together we found a rhythm and it wasn't long before I felt the familiar tightening in my groin. One look at Jade's face, and I knew she was right there with me.

The grand finale of fireworks boomed and burst overhead as together, we found our release in a crashing climax.

Afterward, when the last traces of color in the sky had faded, and the night was once more black, we shared another beer together under the stars. I pointed out various constellations, and listed all the highlights of spending the summer at the lake. Being with Jade was comfortable and in the dark of the night, in the afterglow of amazing sex, it was a little too easy to forget all the reasons we shouldn't be together.

When I drove the boat back to the marina and helped her onto the dock, she gave me a quick hug. "Thank you for showing me the fireworks," she said. "It really was…special. But I should get some rest. I have a meeting in the morning and my to-do list certainly won't take care of itself. Goodnight, Mitch."

Her attitude and tone shifted so quickly, it took me a minute to catch up. When finally I found my words, she'd already hobbled halfway down the dock, toward the great lawn, and away from me and what we'd shared. I wanted to call her back and tell her to hell with being friends, we could make it work being a whole lot more, but instead I let her go. And just for good measure, even though I knew I was being an asshole, I called out after her, "Thanks for the good time, friend."

Chapter Four

JADE

I TOOK one more look in the mirror and adjusted my pressed black slacks and my teal sleeveless blouse that I tucked into my waistband. I smoothed my hair back off my face and examined my makeup. Perfect. Not that I needed to look perfect for my meeting with Gwen, but it was more of a habit than anything else. The need to present myself in a certain way was something my mother had drilled into me. It was a habit that had become exhausting; I couldn't seem to ever let myself relax.

Mitch said something about lake clothes or, more specifically, lake shoes.

Mitch.

Had it really been four days already? Four days since I'd thrown all of my self-imposed rules out the window and slept with him? Again?

It had been four days. Four days for me to self-reflect about that choice. It definitely seemed like a good decision at the time. But there was no point in having regrets. It was just time to move on.

And move on was exactly what I was going to do, because I had so much to do. I had no time for a man in my life, let alone a man like Mitch.

Which was exactly why I needed to stay in control. In this meeting with Gwen, and with everything. I liked being in Cedar Springs. I liked it a lot. But I couldn't make it all work unless I stayed in control.

Satisfied with what I saw in the mirror, I turned away, grabbed my purse and headed out of the restroom to the table where Gwen sat.

"Hey there." Gwen greeted me with a warm smile. "I thought I was early, but here you are in the bathroom the whole time. I should've known." She laughed. It'd become a joke that I wasn't on time unless I was early. It was a joke for Gwen, but that was just the way I lived.

"Sorry," I apologized as I slid into the booth across from Gwen. "I actually meant to be sitting here and possibly have some drinks ordered by the time you got here." I glanced over my shoulder. "Sometimes I wonder if Samantha minds us using her bar as a meeting room. Maybe we should find an actual meeting space?"

Gwen waved her hand in the air, dismissing me. "No way. Sam loves it. As long as we're not taking up tables during the busy time, we're fine. Plus I think she wants mention on the show, or maybe even a cameo." Gwen laughed again.

I loved spending time with Gwen. She was always so happy, it was contagious. But it hadn't always been that way. It wasn't that long ago when Gwen's happiness was tempered with angst. She'd been lying to Ian about who she really was, and that type of deception can really do a number on a girl. But now that everything was out in the open, and had worked out for the better, Gwen was positively glowing. It was great to be around, and the more I was around that, I couldn't help but wonder what it would be like for me to feel that way.

It had to be love. It was the only thing that could put a smile like that on a woman's face. Maybe not the only thing.

No. I was not going to think of Mitch like that, or the way he made me feel, or the smile that he could put on my face. It was time to focus.

"I think we could arrange that," I said, referring to including Samantha in the show. "In fact, maybe she would let us film some scenes in her bar?"

"My bar?" Samantha appeared with a tray in her hand. "I was just coming to see if you girls wanted some drinks, but this conversation sounds more interesting."

Gwen patted the seat next to her, and Sam slid into the booth. "Jade was just worried that you might not be happy with us meeting in your bar all the time."

"Not at all." Sam's smile was genuine, just like she was. The bar and restaurant owner had been one of the first people I had met when I first came to town. And one of the nicest. Not that everyone in Cedar Springs wasn't perfectly welcoming. It really was one of the friendliest places I had ever been. "You guys are totally welcome to meet here."

"That's what I told her," Gwen said. "I promise we won't take up space when it gets busy. Not unless we're here socially, and if that's the case, then you and Trent better be sitting here with us."

"Sounds like a deal to me." Sam slapped her hand on the table. "Now, what can I get you girls to drink?"

I ordered coffee, black, no sugar and Gwen, a green tea. She built her entire brand on the fact that she'd lost a hundred pounds and changed her life. And although I had seen her sneak a treat in once in a while, Gwen was pretty dedicated to her health and fitness, and of course the fans who had built her career.

Once the drinks came, we spent the next forty-five minutes talking about the show: the casting, locations that we were going to use, and of course the script Gwen was working on. I had yet to see a draft, and that was starting to make me nervous. I had no doubt that Gwen would come through, but my control freak was in fine form. We'd never worked on a project quite as big as the one we were dealing with now.

With the last sip of her green tea, Gwen declared the meeting over and put her cup down with force. She put her arms on the table and stared at me. "So are you going to tell me, or am I going to have to pull it out of you?"

I blinked, taken off guard by the change of topic. "What are you talking about?"

Gwen raised her eyebrows and tilted her head. "Mitch."

At the mere mention of his name, my body flushed with heat. I took a deep breath and exhaled slowly, hoping Gwen hadn't noticed the shift in me. "I don't know why you keep asking me about him."

"Right." Gwen rolled her eyes. "I saw the two of you talking the other night. What's going on with you two?"

Right to the point.

If Gwen ever wanted to consider a career change, perhaps investigative reporter or lawyer would be a good choice. She was anything but subtle. With Mitch being Ian's brother, the last thing I needed was any kind of misunderstanding or mix-up. Especially considering there was nothing going on between us. Direct and honest was going to be the best approach. "Nothing," I answered.

Okay, it was *mostly* honest.

"There's no way I believe that." Gwen shook her head. She tried to hide it, but I could see the hurt look in her eyes. We were supposed to be friends. At least, I wanted to be friends, and I was pretty sure Gwen did too.

Being honest was something friends did. Besides, it might be nice to have someone to confide in. I took a breath and let it out slowly. "I wasn't sure if I should say anything…"

"About Mitch?" Gwen sat up at attention, her ponytail swinging behind her. "Because he's Ian's brother?" I nodded slightly. "Don't be silly. We're friends, right?"

The word warmed my heart more than I'd expected it to. I couldn't hide my smile. "We are."

"Good." Gwen reached across the table and took my hand. "Then please don't worry about the fact that they're brothers. It doesn't matter. Not when it comes to this stuff." She gestured between us and took my hand back, clasping them together in front of her. "Now spill. What's going on?"

MITCH

"I CAN'T BELIEVE how busy it is in here, Mitch." Ian snapped the lid of the laptop closed and looked up at me with a grin. "You've done great. I don't know how to say thank-you."

"How about a raise?"

Ian laughed, and I along with him, because up until now, he hadn't paid me anything. I'd volunteered my services, but mostly it was Ian doing me the favor. I definitely didn't need the money, but I did need the fun and relaxed lifestyle that hanging out at the lake afforded me. I needed that a lot.

"Well, you know, whenever you want to, you can take out the boats, or the jet skis…anything. Have a little fun, brother."

My gaze traveled outside to the dock, and my new favorite boat where I had indeed had more than a little fun. "I think that's a good idea." I forced myself to stop thinking about Jade. Again. Canada Day was supposed to be our farewell to fooling around. Friends didn't do that kind of thing.

At least not the type of friends we were supposed to be.

I was turning my attentions to safer waters. Like Evelyn Rose.

"I heard Chelsea set you up on a date?" My brother must have read my mind. Ian handed me a beer and we headed outside to sit in the sun.

"News travels fast." I twisted the cap off my bottle and took a long sip. "And it wasn't so much a setup as a tutoring job."

"Tutoring?"

I nodded. I'd run into Evelyn at Dream Puffs the day after the fireworks, and she'd asked me again if I could please tutor her son. She'd seemed so desperate to get her son up to speed, and I was a sucker for a damsel in distress.

Besides that, she was the epitome of a nice girl and it could only be a good idea to spend time with her. Especially because I needed to get my mind off Jade. "I'm helping out Evelyn's son, Jonah. It's not a big deal. Only a few hours a week. He's a smart kid. It shouldn't take him too long to get caught up."

"Is that all you're helping out with?" Ian nudged me in the ribs. "She's very pretty."

"Agreed." I tipped my bottle back again. I had already decided that when she dropped Jonah off for his first tutoring session, I was going to ask her on a date. After all, you couldn't date a nice girl if you didn't ask. I told my brother as much.

"You're going to ask her out?"

"Why do you sound surprised?" He shouldn't be surprised at any of my dating life. My brother knew me well; he knew I'd always liked the ladies, never gone long without a girlfriend or at the very least, a female friend. The only thing Ian didn't really know was that I was done with superficial relationships. I was ready to grow up.

Ian took a sip of his beer and glanced over at me. "She's not really your type, is she?"

Not really my type? It didn't matter that he was right; it still pissed me off that he would say anything.

"What is my type?" I stared at my brother as I waited for his answer.

Ian chuckled a little, clearly not wanting to say what was on his mind. That in itself was unusual. He never had trouble saying what was on his mind, especially when it came to me.

"It's just that... Evelyn is so..."

"Evelyn is so what?"

Ian put down his beer bottle and turned to face me head on. "She's so damn nice. And while I think she's great, she just doesn't seem like your type."

I didn't know how to feel. I should probably be angry that my big brother didn't think I deserved a nice girl. I could be angry, but he was right. Evelyn wasn't my type. At least she wasn't the type I used to be attracted to. But she was very much the type that I was attracted to now, and I was determined to start over. Try harder. And Evelyn was exactly the type of girl for that.

"You're right. She is damn nice. She's pretty. She's sweet. And not at all what I used to be attracted to. The key word there is used to. But things are different now, and if she says yes, I'd really like to take Evelyn on a date."

Ian didn't say anything. He just picked up his beer bottle and shook his head

"You have something to say, big brother? You might as well just say what's on your mind. We've never had secrets—we shouldn't start now."

"Okay. It's just...what about Jade? I really thought you two were hitting it off. In your snarky, teasing, heightened sexual tension we could all notice, kind of way. I mean, am I wrong?"

He wasn't wrong. He was the opposite of wrong. "We're just friends." It wasn't a lie. That's exactly what we said we'd be. And that's what we were. *Friends*.

"Friends? I don't think I've ever had a friend like that. I mean, you guys... Well, you fooled around, didn't you?"

I hadn't said anything to Ian about the summer solstice or Canada Day. But my brother knew me better than anyone else, so it didn't surprise me. I didn't answer, just raised my eyebrows.

"I knew it." Ian laughed. "The two of you have way too hot of a tension together." His laughter died. "So what the hell? Why are you asking Evelyn on a date, when you clearly have something going with Jade?"

I tipped my beer bottle back to finish the icy-cold drink. I wiped my mouth with the back of my hand and looked at my brother. "Because we're better as friends. Besides, I've been thinking about making a few changes."

"Oh yeah? What kind of changes?"

"I'm thinking about staying in Cedar Springs. I think it's time I settle down. I've actually been thinking about it for a while. Not the Cedar Springs part, but the settling down part. I actually thought that Bethany back in the city might be the one." My stomach turned at the thought. "But that didn't work out." I didn't want to get into the details at the moment. But he already knew the basics that Bethany had cheated on me with the principal, basically made a fool of me in front of the whole school, and totally broke my heart. And here I didn't think I had a heart to break. To my surprise, I was capable of love.

I just needed the right woman.

"I'd be lying if I said that I wasn't surprised." Ian shook his head. "But I think it's great. Really, I do. And if you think Evelyn's the right one, then by all means, the first step would be a date."

His words were encouraging, but I didn't miss the tone of his voice. My brother thought I was crazy. And I knew it had nothing to do with the idea of wanting to settle down. He himself was so goddamn happy now that he'd settled down. No, it had everything to do with my choice of woman.

But there was zero point in trying to convince him otherwise. I would show him; I knew exactly what I needed. A flash of color caught my eye and I turned to see Evelyn and Jonah, holding her hand, walking from the parking lot toward us.

Perfect timing.

I jumped up, dusted off the back of my shorts and walked toward them with a smile.

"Evelyn, it's nice to see you again." I took in her khaki shorts and gauzy flowery top. She looked cute and relaxed with her ponytail and her flip-flops. Perfect for the lake. *Not at all like Jade's big-city outfits.*

I had got to stop thinking about Jade. I focused again on Evelyn and for the first time, the little boy next to her. "You must be Jonah." I offered my hand. The boy took my hand and shook with a surprisingly firm handshake.

"I am," the boy said with confidence. "Mom says you're going to make me smart."

I chuckled and took my hand back. "I have no doubt that you're already quite smart, Jonah. But I'll really do my best to make sure that you know what you're doing in math when school starts this year."

"Thanks. That will make Mom happy." The little boy spoke with wisdom much older than his years. He was like a little man, and I liked him already.

"If it's okay with you, Jonah, I was thinking we could work on that picnic table." I pointed to a grassy area next to the shop where there were a few tables scattered. "I think the sunshine always helps me learn better," I said. Mostly I thought sunshine could only help a little boy. After all, it was summer; the kid didn't need to be cooped up inside more than absolutely necessary. I was a huge believer in summer fun to recharge your batteries.

Jonah readily agreed but looked up at his mom for confirmation. Evelyn smiled and told him of course it would be fine. Seeing a window of opportunity, I sent the kid into the shop to grab himself a soda before the session started, leaving Evelyn and me alone.

"I just wanted to thank you again for helping out Jonah," Evelyn said. Worry lines wrinkled her pretty face. "He really is a smart boy. There's just something about math that he struggles with."

I had seen it before. In fact, from the moment I started teaching, I'd seen it a lot. It only took one teacher, or even one moment, for a child to start believing that they weren't good at math—or anything, really. The doubt could be like a cancer, eating away at their self-esteem, and I knew the only cure was to show them that they could do it. To make them see that they were smart enough, and they always had been. That's exactly what I would do with Jonah.

"Don't worry, Evelyn—"

"Evie," she said. "Please, call me Evie."

"Evie," I said. "Don't worry about a thing. It will only take a few sessions, I'm sure. And Jonah will not only be up to speed with math, he'll be at the top of his class next year."

Evelyn's face lit up with the idea. "How can I thank you? I'll pay you. But honestly, it won't be much. I don't really have a lot of extra money. I just started a little boutique on Main Street, Live, Love, Lake, and all of my money has gone into that. As well as my time." She shook her head and looked away. "There's got to be something I can do to pay you back. You don't happen to need a cute dress, do you?" She laughed and I saw my opportunity.

"Let me take you out. On a date."

Her mouth fell into a little o and her eyes widened. Whatever she was expecting, it hadn't been that. Maybe I had read the situation wrong. Then again, had I read the situation at all?

"A date?" She shook her head a little. "I don't really—"

"Nothing serious," I said quickly. "Let me take you to the Grizzly Paw for a drink. Super casual." I gave her the irresistible McCormick grin. And just as I had expected, Evie's face transformed into a smile of her own and she nodded her consent.

"Okay. Super casual, right?"

"Absolutely. Jonah will be ready to go in about an hour. You want me to bring him up to the shop?"

"No," she said. "Jonah's pretty mature. He can get down the street on his own."

I waited until Evie had walked away, back up the street the way she'd come. I was just about to go find Jonah and begin our session when a familiar voice caught my attention.

My dick twitched in a Pavlovian response.

I shifted my attention to the docks, where Ian now stood with his arm around Gwen, talking to Jade. They must have come over from the Paw, which was why I hadn't seen them on the road.

As if she could sense me watching, Jade turned and spotted me. She waved me over.

It would be the friendly thing to do. To join them and chat about our days. That's what friends did. But Jonah was waiting. I could see the boy, with his books already spread out in front of him on the table. I shook my head and turned toward the picnic tables.

It would only take a minute to say hi. Jonah wouldn't even notice. But it was so much easier not to.

JADE

HE HADN'T SAID HI. I hadn't even seen him wave back. As far as I could see, he hadn't even smiled in my direction. But I wouldn't let it bother me. We were supposed to be friends.

Maybe to Mitch that meant ignoring me. Whatever. That just affirmed that I'd made the right choice.

"I'm sorry. I missed that," I said to Ian. I was aware that I hadn't been listening; hopefully it hadn't been too noticeable.

Gwen gave me a strange look, but fortunately didn't push the matter. "Ian was just saying that he spoke to Cal this morning."

I was instantly at attention. If Cal was interested in playing the role of his older brother, it really would save time when it came to finding an actor who was suitable. Assuming he screen tested well. Not that I even knew what that meant, but it's what the directors told me when I mentioned it. "And what did he say?"

Ian flashed his teeth and wiggled his eyebrows. "He said he'd be on the next flight here. It still feels weird that my little brother wants to play me on TV." He laughed. "Hell, it still feels weird that my life is going to be on TV."

Gwen rubbed his arm and kissed him on the cheek. "Babe, I told you. It's mostly fiction. I mean, it's based on our situation. But it's totally fiction. I'm making it up. But if you're not comfortable…" Gwen looked away, and for a minute I thought she might cry.

Was something going on with her? I knew it had to be a little weird that they were fictionalizing their life for TV, but I just assumed that they were both okay with it. Had that changed?

"Gwen, look at me." Ian tilted her head up so she looked in his eyes. "I told you, it's fine. That doesn't mean it's not a little strange, especially with Cal coming. But honestly, I think it's great. I mean, who better to play me than my brother?"

She nodded. "It's just that… Sometimes… It just seems, well like…"

"Please don't read anything into this. I promise I'll tell you if it's too much. Communication and all that, right?"

I felt a little as though I were intruding on a private moment. Especially when they kissed. But Gwen and Ian didn't seem to care. Probably because they only had eyes for each other. But the second he twisted his hands through Gwen's hair and pulled her mouth to his, I was out of there.

I left the lovebirds on the dock and walked up toward the shop. Mitch had disappeared around the back, and although I told myself I wasn't looking for him, it wouldn't be terrible if I ran into him either.

I moved around the corner but a child's voice stopped me before I walked out of the protection of the building. Then I saw it. Mitch and a little boy sat at a picnic table, with books spread out between them. Mitch was explaining something on a piece of paper, and the little boy was laughing.

I didn't mean to eavesdrop, but at the same time, I didn't move away.

"See? You already knew the answer," Mitch said kindly. "I don't know why your mom told me you were having so much trouble. You're a pretty smart kid."

The boy's face lit up with Mitch's compliment. He clearly knew what he was doing.

"Thanks, Mitch. You make this seem so much easier. I wish you were my teacher."

My heart squeezed in my chest. To have that kind of impact on a child must be amazing. I never had that kind of impact on anyone, let alone someone so impressionable. Watching him gave me a whole new respect for Mitch.

Dammit.

I was supposed to be looking for reasons why Mitch *wasn't* an acceptable man.

Eavesdropping definitely wasn't helping. I tried to back away, but at that moment, my cell phone rang in my purse. Both the boy and Mitch turned to look at me.

Busted.

"Shit," I muttered under my breath before I pasted on an innocent smile and backed around the shop to take the call.

I didn't bother looking at the caller ID before I pressed the Talk button and spoke. "Jade Johnson."

"I'm glad I got you, Jade. Peter Short, here."

Peter was the executive producer of Mr. Summer. Although he'd largely left me alone to make the daily decisions, he didn't reach his level of success by being completely hands-off. I wasn't surprised to hear from him.

"Peter. It's nice to—"

"Jade. We have a problem."

A problem? A shiver of fear passed through me, but only for a moment. I didn't have time for any feelings that would distract me from the ultimate goal. It was a skill I'd perfected years ago: compartmentalizing emotions that had no place in my success.

"What's going on?" My voice was calm and controlled, ready to solve whatever problems had come up.

"It's the script, Jade."

"What about it? Gwen told me this morning—"

"We don't have it yet. I expected it on my desk two weeks ago, but I haven't seen even a rough draft of the pilot."

My stomach clenched. This time, the trace of fear didn't evaporate as before. "But that can't be, Peter." I shook my head even though he couldn't see me. "I was just talking to Gwen and she said—"

"I don't care what she said," Peter interrupted me. "There's no script and without a script, even a draft, there's no show." Peter didn't waste any time getting to the point.

"No, no. I'm sure there was just a misunderstanding." I walked around the shop, toward the docks as I spoke. Maybe Gwen was still there and I could get to the bottom of the situation right away. "In fact," I continued. "Gwen is right here." Sure enough, I spotted the woman in question, still wrapped up in her fiancé's arms, making out in the middle of the dock. I rolled my eyes, even though I was secretly envious of their connection. "I'll go talk to her right now and get to the bottom of it."

"Do that, Jade."

I nodded and then added, "I'm on it. I'm sure it was just a misunderstanding, but I'll make sure you have something in your hand by the end of the day." I wasn't sure I should make such grand promises, especially if Gwen hadn't been totally honest with me, but I needed to say something.

"No. I'm swamped here with other projects," Peter said. "So I'll give you the benefit of the doubt, Jade. I didn't hire you on for this project because I thought I'd need to micromanage you. Take care of this, check the script and make sure it's everything it should be. I'll be in touch. Or it's your career. Got it?"

Did I ever. We spoke for a few more minutes about some of the other details, including casting Cal McCormick to play Ian. It was both a smart choice and a risky one, but even without the screen test, I knew it would be a good decision.

I was both relieved and terrified by the amount of freedom Peter was giving me on this project. Along with Gwen and Ian, there was no one who was closer to the project as I was, and Peter knew that. I wouldn't let him down.

The sooner I got to the bottom of things, the better. I hung up the phone and was just about to track down Gwen, who only a moment ago had left Ian on the dock and was headed up toward the lawn, when Mitch's voice stopped me.

"Were you looking for me?"

I took a moment to compose the look on my face, careful that it was as neutral as it possibly could be. I turned around.

"Hey there." I blatantly ignored his question, and hoped he wouldn't call me on it.

I tried not to stare at him. How was it possible that a man

could look so damn sexy wearing nothing but baggy khaki shorts and a tight-fitted T-shirt? a

Easy. It was possible because he was Mitch. And he was sexy. It didn't help that I knew exactly what hid under that thin piece of cotton.

I cleared my throat and looked away out to the lake. That didn't help either, because every time I looked at the lake I couldn't help but remember what we had done out there only a few nights ago.

"Is it busy today? I was hoping to talk to Gwen. Maybe I should get going." I glanced in the direction Gwen had disappeared and turned to leave, but he grabbed my arm.

"What's the rush?"

I turned around again and immediately wished I hadn't. Mitch's eyes traveled up and down my body, taking in my outfit, taking me in. His eyes on me made me want to tremble, but I swallowed hard to maintain my composure.

"There is just so much to do with the show." I hoped I was keeping my tone light and friendly. I pulled my purse higher up on my shoulder. "Besides, it's a beautiful day. You must be crazy busy."

Mitch took a step back and tucked his hands in his pockets. "It is. But all the boats are out and Chelsea's helping with jet skis. And I was just finishing up a tutoring session. So I have a few minutes. If you do."

"Tutoring? Seems an awful lot like teaching. I thought you were taking a break?"

"Once a teacher, always a teacher. Besides that, it was hard to say no to his mom."

I glanced over his shoulder, where the boy was packing up his books. I still didn't know a lot of people in town, but I'd seen the boy and his mom on Main Street at the bakery the other day. I remembered because he had been a nice kid, and had taken my empty dishes for me. "His mom is Evelyn Rose, right?"

Mitch nodded.

A lump formed in my chest, which was entirely stupid. Because I had no claim to him. And just because he was tutoring her kid didn't mean anything was going on between them. And even if it was... "She's very pretty."

A look a lot like guilt flashed over Mitch's face, and I decided I didn't want to press the issue. I didn't want to know whether anything was going on between them. It was easier that way.

"Well, I should go. I do have a lot of work to do." Once again, I turned to walk away, only this time I managed to get a few steps in.

"Jade. Wait."

I swallowed hard and put my smile back on my face before I turned around.

"You can't possibly be working all the time, right? I mean, as your friend, I think it's my duty to show you a little summer fun, too. Wouldn't you agree?"

I should say no. But I was tired of saying no to anything that was fun. Everyone around me was having a good time, and it was summer after all, and I was in a lake town. "I'd like that. You did promise me a boat ride during the day, in the sunshine." Something flashed in his eyes, and I knew he was remembering exactly what had gone on in the boat at night. "As friends."

"As friends," he agreed with a smile. "Wednesday? Ten in the morning."

"I can make that work." I turned to leave, this time for real. But his voice stopped me one more time.

"And Jade? Go get yourself some lake clothes."

Chapter Five

MITCH

ONE OF THE best parts about summer for me were the longer days. Especially when I was at the lake and could enjoy them to their fullest. I walked out onto the deck of the old cabin, put my hands on the wooden rail, and gazed out over the lake.

I had to admit, when Ian first told me I was coming back to Cedar Springs to open up the cabin, I'd had my reservations. After all, a lot went down in Cedar Springs. A lot that shaped our whole lives.

I let my eyes travel to the water's edge and the big old tree where we used to swing from a rope into the water. An old frayed rope still hung there, but there was no way I was going to swing on it now. Maybe after it had been replaced. Maybe that's something I could do.

I laughed to myself, remembering how Declan, only eight, had tried to prove to his older brothers that he was big enough to do what we did. We probably shouldn't have let the younger boys try, but Declan was never one to be talked out of things. Of course it resulted in Declan not letting go of the rope when he was supposed to, causing him to slam into the trunk of the tree, fall to the ground and break his arm. Which then resulted in Ian and me getting in trouble. Of course, it also meant that summer kinda sucked for Dec. If you didn't count all the ice cream and treats he got from Mom.

Yes, there were a lot of memories at the lake. But not all of them were great.

It had been at the lake where our whole life had fallen apart. Our mother had taken us up for the summer, just as she always did. Our father was set to join us for the celebrations, just the way he always did. Everything about that summer when I was eighteen had been normal, except my dad had come to the cabin early to break the news to me that he had another family and was leaving us. It was the night of the summer solstice, the night it all changed.

That had been the last time I'd been to Cedar Springs. With Ian's help mostly, our mother had packed up and we'd gone back to the city so she could find work and try to put our life back together again.

I tipped my head up to the sky and took a deep breath. It seemed like a lifetime ago when all that happened. How things had changed since. The biggest change, of course, was that Chelsea was in our lives.

If anyone had asked me five years ago if I ever wanted to get to know my little half-sister, the product of my father's affair, I would have laughed in their face. Now, of course, after only knowing her for a short time, I couldn't imagine things without her. I was looking forward to meeting Amber, our other sister, as well.

Things definitely had changed. But the one thing that had remained the same was the way being at the lake made me feel. For the first time in longer than I could remember, I felt like myself again. My hand reached up and scratched the scruff on my chin. Not that growing a beard was the epitome of who I was, but it was a symbol. Working at the stuffy private school for the last few years, public perception had been extremely important. I had to watch everything I did, because everyone else was watching. It was exhausting.

I breathed in the fresh air coming off the lake and let it out in a long sigh.

"Looks like I may be interrupting something."

I turned around and greeted Chelsea with a smile. "Not at all. I was just standing out here, remembering."

She came to join me at the rail, crossed her arms and leaned her head down, looking out at the water. "You know, I envy you guys. That you grew up with all this. Must've been a great childhood, you know, until…"

I'd never talked to Chelsea about our parents, or more specifically, our father. There'd be a time for it, but it wasn't right now.

"Well, I'm glad you're here now," I said. "Everyone should have a lake in their life."

Chelsea nodded. "I totally agree with that." We stood in silence for a few moments, enjoying the view, listening to the birds, and watching the boats in the distance slip by on the lake in the late afternoon, when suddenly Chelsea stood. "I totally forgot," she said. "Ian just told me that Cal is coming later today, or I should say in the middle of the night. I mean, I guess his flight gets in…but we probably won't see him—"

"Until tomorrow?" I laughed at her excitement.

Unlike Ian and me, my younger two brothers and my half-sisters had grown up as friends. It had more to do with them being close in age than anything else, and perhaps the fact that Ian and I were too damn stubborn for our own good. "I can't wait to see him," I said genuinely.

It had been way too long since I'd seen my little brother. Cal had been so busy in Australia working as a model, and apparently a little bit as an actor, that he hadn't had much time to come home and visit his family. It didn't hurt that he was dating one of the hottest new actresses on TV.

Bridget Murphy was a star of the hit lifeguarding show that had been filming in Australia for the last two months and Cal had been photographed by her side on a number of occasions. And they were a good-looking couple.

Another couple.

I tried not to let it bother me that my little brother had also found love, while I was still looking. "I wonder what his girl-friend thinks about him coming all the way over here, for a show of his own?"

"Didn't you hear?"

"Hear what?"

"They broke up." Chelsea bit her lip and opened her eyes wide in fake horror. "I don't know what happened, but I think it was Cal who broke up with her. You think he's losing his mind?"

I shook my head and laughed. "I'm sure we'll hear all about it when he gets here tomorrow. What time is it?" I changed the subjects. I had my date with Evelyn tonight, and I didn't want to be late. It had taken enough convincing to get her to go out with me as it was. The last thing I needed was to be late.

"It's just after five. Why? What's up?"

I shrugged casually. "Just heading to the Grizzly Paw. You're not working tonight?"

"Nope. I've got the night off. And I'm looking forward to a little bit of couch time. It's long overdue."

I gave my sister a kiss on the forehead, said good-bye, and left her on the deck.

I was looking forward to tonight.

Over the last few days, I tutored Jonah twice more. He was a smart kid, and he was catching on fast. It was true: you could take the teacher out of the school, but you couldn't take the school out of the teacher.

I laughed at myself, not entirely sure that made sense. But regardless, I was excited to tell Evelyn how well her son was doing. I was pretty sure it would make her smile. And she had a pretty smile.

An image of Jade's sexy smile flashed in my mind, almost knocking me to my knees with the power of it.

I'd been trying for the life of me, but I could not get thoughts of that woman out of my head. I was really hoping focusing on another woman, a woman as great as Evie, would be just the distraction I needed. Because I definitely needed something.

JADE

I HAD BEEN PUTTING it off long enough. That morning, I'd taken a long, hard look in my closet and had faced facts. As much as I didn't want to admit it, Mitch was right. I needed some lake clothes. My wardrobe was full of black, tailored pants and structured blouses. That might work for the city for negotiating contracts and deals. But more and more, I was finding my wardrobe was not entirely practical for life at the lake.

I'd already decided today would be the day that I'd go down to Main Street to check out the new boutique. Evelyn's boutique. The fact that Mitch was tutoring Evelyn's son had definitely been a factor in the reason I'd put off my shopping trip until now.

Despite the fact that I kept telling myself it didn't matter. But even if that didn't bother me a little bit, the reality was there weren't that many places to shop in Cedar Springs, so regardless of the little seed of jealousy I felt in the pit of my stomach, I didn't have a choice. I was going to have to check out the shop.

At least I thought it was just a seed of jealousy that was making my stomach so upset. For the last few days, I felt as if I might be coming down with something, but besides an upset stomach that only seemed to respond to peppermint tea, there were no other symptoms. I must just be a little run-down, which didn't make much sense considering I'd never felt more relaxed and at peace in my life. The lake did that.

Just walking down Main Street relaxed me. Everyone was so friendly. They all waved at me. They even said hello, calling me by name. It was so unlike anything I was used to. I'd barely been there a month, but already I'd been accepted as a local.

I paused before opening the door to the Live, Love, Lake boutique. I'd purposely waited the whole day, planning my arrival only a few minutes before closing time so I wouldn't have to stay long.

Bells jingled as I opened the door.

Cute.

In fact, the whole store was cute. At least that was my first impression. There were racks of casual, soft colored clothes made of cotton and other flowing fabrics. There wasn't a pair of black slacks in sight.

I stood, slightly dazed, in the doorway and looked around. I was just about to turn around and leave, when a voice stopped me.

"Hello. Can I help you?" A pretty petite woman, wearing a floral sundress that probably came off one of her racks, appeared from the back room. *Evelyn.*

I shook my head, and almost told the woman no. But I needed clothes. "Yes. I really hope you can."

Evelyn's smile was sweet, just like she was. I didn't even need to talk to her to know that she was a lovely person. Some people just radiated a genuine kindness. Evelyn was definitely that type of person. "I'm going to close in about fifteen minutes," she said. "But don't worry about that. How can I help you? What were you looking for exactly?"

I took a step inside the store, feeling much more at ease. "Everything. I've been told that if I'm going to spend the summer at the lake, I should probably dress down a little." I held my arms out and laughed at myself. "And I guess that's probably true."

"Well, I think you look great. But I can definitely help you choose a few pieces that would probably be more appropriate for hanging out at the lake. Why don't we start over here?" Evelyn led me toward the back of the store and a rack of shorts. "The first thing you're going to need is a good pair of shorts. Something casual, but still something with a little bit of structure, more like what you're used to."

The more she spoke, the more I liked her. She couldn't be more opposite than myself, but one thing I could appreciate was a woman of business. And Evelyn clearly knew her business.

"My name is Evelyn, by the way. But most people call me Evie. I've seen you around town. You're working on the show with Gwen and Ian, right?"

"Guilty. But lucky me, I get to spend the summer in Cedar Springs. My name is Jade. Jade Johnson."

Instead of shaking my hand, Evie offered me another warm smile. "Well, it's really nice to meet you, Jade. Let's find you some clothes."

With amazing effectiveness, Evie pulled pieces off the racks and handed them to me in the changing room. Almost every item Evie gave me looked great. Obviously, the clothes were different than what I was used to but Evie had an eye for picking items close to what I was used to, only much more appropriate for the lake. I was surprised when only twenty minutes later, I had a pile of new wardrobe choices.

"I can't thank you enough." I took the pile of clothes to the counter in the back of the store. "You really do have beautiful things here. And honestly, I'm not sure if you noticed, but I was a little out of my depth in here. I really appreciate your help."

"It's my pleasure." Evie started scanning tags into the till and folding the pile of clothes. "I've only just opened this season, and it's nice to see the community responding so positively. It's always been my dream to open a shop in my hometown. And frankly, it's taken about all my energy. But it's so worth it."

"Well," I said, "if my experience has been any indication, you're going to do great. I don't think I've ever bought so many clothes in such a short time, and it was relatively painless. I think I have an outfit for every occasion in here, unless of course I need a cocktail dress of some sort." I laughed. I couldn't imagine a situation where I might need a cocktail dress in Cedar Springs. "But I think—"

"Oh, my God!" Evie dropped the blouse she was folding and looked up. "I have just the thing. It just came in. You have to try it on."

I shook my head. "I was just kidding. I don't need a fancy dress. I already have a few cute sundresses here." I patted the pile of clothes on the counter. I already had more than enough. "Honestly, I'm fine."

"You don't have to buy it. But you have to try it on. It will look so good on you. Just wait right here."

Evie was so excited and she'd been so helpful, it was the least I could do. A moment later, Evie reappeared with a stunning dress in her hand. It both fit with the rest of the clothes in the store, and at the same time was incredibly different. I disappeared into the changing room and slipped the dress over my head. I didn't even look in the mirror before going to show Evie, who waited impatiently for the reveal.

"You are gorgeous. That dress is absolutely amazing on you. I wasn't sure if I should order it—it's not really something that most people around here would buy. But on you, it's incredible. What do you think?"

I turned toward the mirror and drew in a breath. The dress was amazing. The emerald-green color made my eyes pop and was made even more dramatic by my dark hair falling over my bare shoulders. The fabric hugged my body, over my breasts, my waist, and my hips before falling into a light and floaty skirt. I shook my hips back and forth, letting the fabric float around my knees. It really was beautiful. "It's stunning."

"I knew it would be perfect on you."

It was perfect. Not that I had anywhere to wear it. But it really did feel like the dress was made just for me. I took a minute and stood in front of the mirror, assessing my image. I ran my hands down my sides and over my stomach to my hips.

What the...

I stopped and raised my hands up to my stomach again. My normally flat belly felt bloated and round. I spun to the side to examine my reflection. Then the other side.

"Is something wrong?" Evie looked concerned as she watched me. "Is it the dress? It looks fantastic on you...but don't worry. You don't have to buy it."

"Oh, no," I said quickly. "It's not that at all. And I'd totally buy it if I had anywhere to wear it. It's just..." I ran my hands over my stomach again. "It must be the fresh air or maybe I've just been enjoying too many wings at the Grizzly Paw." I laughed. "I've definitely put on a few pounds. I'll have to join Gwen in a workout later this week."

And skip the wings next time I'm at the Paw. Now that I bought a full new wardrobe, I didn't want to eat my way out of it right away. I let my hands slide slowly over the bump one more time.

It was definitely too many wings. Right?

Quickly, I did some mental math.

There was no—

"Well, I think you look great. Your stomach is perfectly flat." Evie laughed, interrupting me from my thoughts that were becoming a little too disturbing. "Thanks for trying it on for me. I just knew it would look amazing on you."

"No problem." I smiled, forcing the troubling thoughts out of my head. "I would totally buy it if I weren't already getting so much. What's the damage? I should probably get going so you can get out of here." I'd been having such a good time shopping—something in and of itself I never thought I'd do—that I'd totally forgotten that I'd gone into the store so close to closing time. "I'm so sorry," I said. "You probably have something to do. I'll get changed."

I went quickly into the changing room and slipped out of the pretty dress, slightly disappointed that I wouldn't be taking it home with me. Bloated stomach and all, it still looked great. And it did have enough stretch that if I kept getting bigger... Not that I *would* keep getting bigger! I couldn't let myself think that way.

I'd just been eating too many wings. And that was easily remedied. I made a snap decision to include the dress with my purchases as well. I may not have anywhere to wear it at the moment, but maybe if I had the dress, the opportunity would arise. Plus, it would be good incentive to work out and get rid of my tummy.

I laughed at myself and handed Evie the dress. "I'll take this one, too."

"I knew it." For a moment, I thought Evie might actually squeal with excitement. She really was good at what she did. Looking at my bill, I thought, maybe she was a little *too* good at it.

"Thank you so much, Jade. You are officially one of my

first customers." Evie handed me two big bags full of clothes. "And I had a great time getting to know you."

"Me too," I said, and I meant it.

We walked together to the door. "Again, I'm really sorry if I kept you too long."

Evie waved away my concern. "It's no biggie. I actually do have a date." She held up her fingers in air quotes. "But between you and me, I'm pretty sure it's not a match. I mean, Mitch is a great guy, but he's just—"

"Mitch McCormick?" As if it were any other Mitch. After all, he was tutoring Evie's son. The seed of jealousy in the pit of my stomach sprouted and took root.

"Yes." Evie's face flushed with embarrassment. "Of course, you must know Mitch. Please don't...it's not that he's not a great guy, but...Well, I probably shouldn't say anything until I've gone out with him, right?"

I nodded mechanically. "Right." I forced a smile and reached for the door.

Logically, I had no right to be jealous or have any feelings one way or the other about Mitch or his dating life.

We're just friends.

Right.

And it's just too many wings.

My internal voice startled me into stopping short in the middle of the sidewalk.

What the hell?

It *was* too many wings. I'd been lazy since arriving in Cedar Springs. That's all it was.

I looked up at the storefront I'd stopped in front of, The General Store.

But maybe...buying a pregnancy test wouldn't hurt.

I knew I was being stupid and paranoid and totally ridiculous. But still, I shifted my purchases into one hand and pulled the door of the General Store open.

MITCH

FRIDAY NIGHTS at the Grizzly Paw could get busy, especially in the summer. I had gone early enough to get us a table that was at least a little bit out of the way so we might have a chance to talk and get to know each other. I positioned myself so I could see the door, and Evie, when she came in.

She was late. It wasn't a big deal, though; she sent me a quick text to let me know that she had a last-minute customer at the shop, and I knew what it was like to have a new business. I would have been late too.

The Paw started to fill up, both with locals and summer people. It was a weird thing to be both a summer person and a local.

Growing up, I'd always been a summer person. Even after spending almost sixteen summers in a row, me and my brothers were still considered summer people. We were temporary. But that hadn't stopped us from making friends. Every summer, we'd meet a few more people. Until it finally felt as if we were locals. At least we acted like locals. I had to chuckle, thinking that everyone else probably disagreed.

Ever since Ian had come back to town and set up a business, the McCormicks had officially been given local status. And all of our summer friends, at least the ones who hadn't moved away, had finally accepted us as such.

I sipped my beer and watched the door. While I waited, I'd been making a mental list of things to talk about with Evie. I hadn't gotten very far. Not beyond telling her how Jonah was doing with his math. How was it that I couldn't find any common ground between us? She was a young, beautiful, single mom and a business owner; I should have a lot to talk to her about. But maybe not as much in common as I'd originally hoped.

But I was still going to try. Just as soon as she showed up.

"Hey, man." Rhys Anderson, one of the local police officers, one of my old friends from my summers, stopped in front of my table with his girlfriend Kari Fox next to him. "Are you waiting for someone? It's pretty busy in here already."

"Actually, I'm waiting for my date."

"Oh." Kari perked up with a smile. "You're dating Jade Johnson, aren't you? I don't know her very well yet, but Gwen sure talks highly of her. And Deanna wanted to invite her to her next book club night. Do you think she'd like that?"

"We're actually not dating."

Kari's face fell, and she instantly looked mortified. "I'm so sorry." She glanced over to Rhys, who only shrugged. "I guess I just thought... I saw you guys at the festival... And then of course, at the Canada Day celebrations. I'm sorry. I didn't mean to assume anything."

I smiled kindly. It did seem to be a mistake more and more people were making. "It's fine," I said. "We're friends. And if it helps, I do think she'd probably like a book club. But I'm not really sure if she has time to read."

Rhys laughed and interrupted. "That's perfect," he said. "Because I don't actually think they do a whole lot of reading at book club."

Kari scowled and smacked her boyfriend lightly on the arm, but then laughed. Rhys pulled her close. He gave her a quick kiss on the forehead. "You have no idea what goes on there, and it makes you crazy."

"Maybe so," Rhys admitted. "But I do know I've never seen you reading one of the books."

Kari shook her head again and turned her attention to me. "Well, if you think that Jade would like to be part of it, we'd love to have her. Deanna is kind of in charge, but I'll let her know that you think she'd be interested."

Deanna was Gwen's oldest friend, and a longtime local in Cedar Springs, after returning from a stint away in medical school. She was also the only doctor in town these days, and therefore pretty busy. When she wasn't working, she was usually with her boyfriend Marcus, a professional snowboarder who had recently started his own line of custom snowboards. The more I thought about it, there were a lot of new businesses going on in Cedar Springs. It really was becoming more and more of a happening place.

More the reason to stay.

"We probably shouldn't keep you." Rhys started to steer Kari away from the table. "After all, if you're waiting for your date, we don't want to cramp your style. Are you going to let us know who it is?"

"Don't be nosy, Rhys. Mitch will let us know if he wants to." She wiggled her eyebrows at me, and I laughed. "So do you want to?"

I knew better than to know there'd be any secrets in Cedar Springs, which was obvious enough by the fact that everyone thought I was dating Jade. But I was saved from having to tell them who I was waiting for by the arrival of my date herself. "Here she is now."

Both of my friends' heads turned at the same time toward the door. It was Kari's head that snapped back first. "Evelyn Rose? You're meeting Evelyn for a date? But she's...and you..."

I wasn't sure what that meant, or how I should feel about it. But I didn't have time to ask; I'd already waved at Evie, and she was coming over.

"I'm so sorry I'm late." She smiled apologetically before she greeted Rhys and Kari. "Hi, guys. It's good to see you."

"Hi, Evie," Kari said. "We were just leaving to get our own table. But we just wanted to say hi."

Before anyone could say anything else, Rhys and Kari were gone. Evie looked to me with a question in her eyes. "Did I say something?"

I stood and waited until Evie had sat before I sat back down. "It's not you. They just didn't want to interrupt. I'm glad you made it. Busy day?"

For the next few minutes, Evie and I shared easy conversation about our days. Evie lit up when she started to talk about her new shop, Live, Love, Lake. I learned that after becoming a single mom, she had to figure out a way to support herself and her son in a town with very few options. At least up until recently. With the opening of the new exclusive Springs resort and the reopening of the ski hill Stone Summit, the town of Cedar Springs had experienced a rebirth of sorts, providing a wealth of new opportunity if you were ready.

Evie had been ready.

The more I learned about her, the more impressed I was with her and her determination to make a better life for her son. The conversation segued easily from her new shop to Jonah and the tutoring I was providing. I'd been waiting all day to tell her how well Jonah was doing, how much he was picking up on.

Just as I had suspected, it wasn't that the child didn't understand math; he just hadn't been responding to his teacher. After only a few tutoring sessions with him, Jonah was more than caught up. In fact, I suspected he'd be at the head of his class come September.

"I don't know how to thank you, Mitch." Evie reached across the table and grabbed my hand, and seeming to realize what she had done, she released it quickly. "I mean, I wish I could help him with everything he needs. But between trying to get this shop off the ground and just… Well, just everything.

There just doesn't seem to be enough time. By the time I realized he was falling behind, it was already the end of the school year."

"Don't worry about it, Evie. I was happy to help. I totally understand—well, not totally. I mean, I don't understand what it would be like to be a single mom. Beyond the fact that my own mother was."

"Oh." Evie got that look on her face that most people got when they remembered the great McCormick scandal of ten years ago when our family had disappeared from Cedar Springs due to personal problems. The last thing I wanted was Evie's pity, or worse, any awkwardness about it. "Oh Mitch, I'm sorry. I forgot—"

"No." I cut her off. "All that stuff is in the past. The McCormicks are back. And everything is different now."

I used the opportunity to wave the waitress over and order new drinks. When she'd gone, Evie crossed her arms on the table in front of her and leaned in. "Are you all back?" she asked. "I mean, I know you and Ian are here, but...are your other brothers here too?"

Something about the way she asked got my attention. Evie was younger than me, and I'd only known of her in the vaguest sense when I was a teenager, so if she was friendly with one of my other brothers, I didn't know about it. "Do you know them? Declan and Cal, I mean."

She blushed and her pretty face turned a vivid shade of pink. She looked down at the table and the napkin she was worrying between her fingers. "No." She shook her head, still not looking up. "I mean, not really. I knew of them, though. I knew *of* all of you. But I was a few years younger, so I didn't go to the parties..."

I chuckled. The longer I sat and spoke with her, the more I realized what a nice girl Evie was. And yes, I'd been looking for a nice girl. But there was no spark between us, even if I really wanted there to be. But I couldn't even be sure that was true anymore. And it was clear that Evie felt the same way.

"Declan is out saving the world somewhere, so I don't think he'll be back."

"Oh." Her disappointment was obvious and she didn't even try to hide it.

"But Cal will be here tomorrow."

Her head shot up, delight on her face. "Cal? I heard he was in Australia."

"Don't tell me you read about him in the magazines?"

"Guilty," she said. "Don't tell anyone—gossip magazines are my guilty pleasure. It's really pretty embarrassing."

I shrugged. "We all have our guilty pleasures." Some of those things were more pleasurable than others. But I was definitely not going to get into that with Evie.

Their drinks arrived and we spent the rest of the evening chatting comfortably with the awareness that we would only be friends. We didn't even have to discuss it, which was how I knew we could really be friends.

If only it could be that easy with Jade.

Chapter Six

JADE

I HAD GIVEN myself the weekend to be shocked. I had given myself two full days to hide in my rented house, lie on the couch, and stare at the pregnancy test. For two whole days, I barely ate, drank only peppermint tea, and held that little plastic stick in my hand without fully registering what I was looking at.

Pregnant.

How was it even—no. I *knew* how it was possible. It's just that it shouldn't have been possible.

The night of the summer solstice festival. It had to have been then. But I was on the Pill. I'd been on the Pill since I was sixteen years old. But I had just finished a round of antibiotics for a minor ear infection. That had to have been it.

But things like that only happened in the movies.

Except that wasn't true.

It was happening to me.

I'd given myself the weekend. And on Monday, I woke up, showered, dressed in one of my new outfits—not too casual, not too formal—grabbed my laptop, and walked down to Main Street to Dream Puffs bakery. I decided not to think about the positive pregnancy test. Just long enough to get some work done. It's not as though I could ignore it forever. Obviously, I would have to deal with it. But one thing I did need was some control. And the only way I could think to do that was to work.

But my brain had other ideas. I spent most of that Monday not opening any of the files I needed to look at, not making any of the phone calls to clients I needed to make, but instead surfing the Internet.

False positive test. Signs of early pregnancy. Not really pregnant. How soon can you tell?

I typed in every variation of every search topic I could think of. And by the end of the day, I had read more personal experiences of how women just "knew" they were pregnant right away. Apparently, some women just had a feeling. Other women started to show within two weeks. One woman talked about immediate food cravings. Another, about how her breasts were sore the day after she conceived.

I also learned that pregnancy tests were very accurate, some of them even able to determine pregnancy before a missed period, but the only way to really know for sure was to see your doctor.

I only knew of one doctor in town. Deanna Gordon. Who happened to be Gwen's best friend, and a very nice person. In fact, she was a person I could see myself being friends with. And was that the type of person I wanted diagnosing my unwanted pregnancy?

Unwanted. My hand instantly went to my stomach, to the very slight—only I could actually tell—swell there. No, maybe not entirely unwanted.

But first things first. I made a call to Doctor Deanna Gordon and an hour later, I found myself sitting in a thin paper gown on the exam table across from a woman I'd recently shared drinks with.

Oh God, I drank!

Deanna smiled warmly in an effort, I was sure, to put me at ease. It didn't work. I couldn't wait one more moment.

"Well?" I asked. "What did the test say?"

Before changing into my gown, I had peed in a cup and left it with a nurse.

Deanna opened her mouth, but before she could say anything, I cut her off. "Wait. Don't tell me. I know it's positive. I mean, I don't know, know. But I know. You know?" Aware I wasn't making any sense, I took a deep breath and tried again. "Am I pregnant?"

"Yes."

I'd expected to feel something. Shock. Excitement. Sadness. I didn't feel anything. Not at first anyway.

"How do you feel? Do you have any symptoms yet? It is still pretty early, but there must've been a reason you took the test. Have you missed a period already?"

Deanna's questions came at me in what felt like a flurry, despite the fact that the other woman spoke slowly and calmly. All at once, the reality of what I'd just been told kicked in.

"Jade?" Deanna stood at my side with her hand on my arm, but I only barely registered that fact. "Maybe you should lie down." It wasn't a question. Deanna helped lower my back on the exam table so that I was lying on my side with my legs tucked up under me. "Take some deep breaths. Just give it a minute to let the news sink in. I take it this wasn't entirely planned?"

The question struck me as funny, because Deanna didn't know me well but she knew me well enough to know that I wasn't with anyone. In fact, she may not even know that I had been with Mitch. But due to the circumstances, she must know that I'd been with *someone* at some point. "You could say it's a bit of a surprise."

"Don't worry. There are lots of options, no matter what it is that you decide to do. And I know we're friendly and it's a small town. But I just want you to know that I'm very discreet. Whatever happens in this office will stay here. I hope that puts your mind at ease a little."

I nodded and sat up. I felt better. The initial shock or realization—or whatever it was that had just washed over me—was gone. "I appreciate that," I said. "And it is a surprise, of course. I mean, I've had a few days to get used to the idea. I know those tests are pretty accurate now. But hearing it from you, it just seems so much more…"

"Real?"

"Yes. Real. And I guess I have some decisions to make." Even as I said that, I knew there weren't a lot of decisions to make. The baby might not be planned, but that didn't mean I couldn't make it work. If that's what I wanted.

Deanna nodded and wrote something on a clipboard before she sat back down on her stool. "Well, no matter what decision you make, you should start taking some prenatal vitamins. At least for now. And I'd like to see you back here in a few weeks. Just to discuss things."

"Okay."

"And Jade? As a friend, if you need to talk…or if you need anything, just let me know. Also, a good friend of mine, Cynthia—she owns the General Store—she went through something similar. In fact, her baby was just born a few months ago, but they're doing well. She might be a good one to talk to."

The last thing I wanted to do was talk to anybody, at least not until I figured things out myself. At the very least, I probably should tell Mitch first.

Mitch.

What was he going to think? What was he going to say?

It wouldn't change anything between us, because there was nothing there to change. But still.

After I left the doctor's office, I spent the rest of the day walking around town. It was a beautiful summer day and I soaked it all in. I walked up and down Main Street. I watched the mothers with their children: ice cream cones, sticky hands, scraped knees, and baby strollers.

Did I want that? Could that be me?

I strolled the side streets, lined with trees in front of cute little houses with flowers planted in the gardens. Most of the front lawns had bikes and toys strewn all over them, evidence to the young family inside.

Cedar Springs was a great place to raise a child. A family. I could be a family. Just me and the baby. After all, I had been raised by a single mother. And although I wasn't about to use my mother for any parenting examples, it was possible. And in a town like Cedar Springs, that was so friendly and close, so filled with love, I would have support. I could do it.

I could be a single mom. I could give my baby the type of childhood I wished I had had.

My hands went to my stomach. I could do all of that.

Couldn't I?

MITCH

"I DON'T KNOW why Cal had to drive himself." Ian paced on the driveway before he spun around and stared at me, where I reclined in one of the old wooden chairs next to the front door. We'd been outside for close to thirty minutes waiting for our little brother to show up. Late. As usual. This time by days, instead of hours. "We could have gone into the

city to pick him up," Ian continued. "Then he wouldn't
be so——"

"Late? Of course he would." I laughed at my brothers'
predictable natures. Not much had changed. Cal, as the
youngest, was known for not considering how his schedule may
or may not affect others, and it still made Ian crazy. "Relax," I
said. "He'll be here when he gets here. And about that—where
were you thinking we'd all sleep?"

Our old cabin was roomy. It had to be, with four boys
running around. But we'd grown up with bunkbeds, and
although I was all for having everyone under one roof, there
was only so much space, and sharing a room with my adult
brothers was considerably different than when we were kids.
Especially if I wanted to have a grown-up sleepover.

Not that there was much chance of that. At least not with
Evie because we'd decided to be friends. Real friends. And...
well, I'd decided to be just be friends with Jade, too. But that
was different.

"You and Cal can share for now," Ian said. "No?"

That had to be the arrangement, because Ian and Gwen
had taken over the master suite, Chelsea was in the younger
boys' room, and I had reclaimed my old bunk. "For now." I
shrugged. "Sure. But what happens when——"

"You have a girl over?"

"That's not what I was going to say, but..."

"Let me know when you have a girl." My brother taunted
me, and if he hadn't been standing so far away, I probably
would have punched him in the arm.

"What about when Dec comes?" I changed the subject,
choosing not to focus on my current lack of female companionship. "We can't all squeeze into one room. We're grown
men, for God's sake."

"When's Dec coming? Have you talked to him?"

"No." I had to admit, I hadn't. Not lately anyway. But I

knew my little brother, and I knew if we were all gathering at the lake after so many years, he wouldn't be far behind. There was nothing Declan loved more than family, except maybe his memories of the lake. He'd be here eventually. And we both knew it.

Ian nodded. "I know. He'll be here soon. I guess I haven't really thought about where we'd all—"

Ian couldn't finish his thought because the sound of a very loud, very expensive car coming up the road pulled our attention away.

"Cal's here." I pushed up from the chair to join my older brother, right as the brightest, orangest BMW convertible flew around the corner into the driveway. "Do you think he could find a brighter car?" I nudged Ian in the side and we both shook our heads.

The car came to a screeching halt, and true to form, Cal skipped over using the door and hopped out of the car, looking every bit the international male model that he was in his skinny jeans, tight T-shirt, and mirrored sunglasses. "Hey. I like the welcoming committee."

"Keeping it real, I see, brother." I pulled Cal into a hug, slapped his back and released him to greet Ian the same way. "Interesting choice of rental."

"This?" Cal ran his hand along the hood of the car. "It's no rental. Now that I'm finally going to be an actor on a hit show, it's about time I started acting like one."

"Whoa." Ian held up his hands. "First of all, we *hope* it will be a hit show. Second, starting salaries are usually pretty modest. And third, you didn't officially get the job yet."

I laughed. "Since when have little details like that stopped our brother?"

"Right?" Cal shrugged. "Don't worry. I have a ton saved from my modeling jobs and the royalties aren't going to dry up anytime soon. Besides, I need wheels to get around, right?"

Ian shook his head, and I laughed again. "I like it that everything has stayed the same. It's good to see you, Cal."

"It's good to be here." He put his hands on his hips and breathed in the fresh air. "Man, it's been a long time. Too long."

Behind him, Ian had a satisfied smile on his face. I knew how important it was to my older brother to bring this back to us. None of us realized how much we missed the lake until Ian came back to reopen things up.

But now that we had it back, I knew it wasn't going to go anywhere again.

We walked inside. Cal left his suitcase by the front door and we went straight out to the back deck, where we each grabbed a beer in a toast.

"To summer," Cal said.

"Summer."

"Brothers," I added.

We drank deeply and spent a few moments in silence, looking out over the lake.

"Damn, it's good to be back," Cal said. "Australia has some nice beaches and of course the ocean is amazing, but there is nothing like this." He shook his head in wonderment and gazed off into the distance.

Ian and I exchanged looks. I couldn't remember ever seeing my little brother so reflective. "So...Cal...what's up?" I asked.

"What do you mean?" He turned and leaned on his elbows.

"What are you doing here?" Ian asked. "I mean, what are you *really* doing here?"

Cal looked between us, clearly trying to assess what we were after. "I'm here for the show." He focused on Ian. "Your show. Besides, even if I wasn't, can't a guy come home now and then?"

"Of course," I said. "But this is different. Things were going so well in Australia. I mean, judging by the car in the driveway, they were going really well. Why mess with it?"

Cal shrugged. "Bigger and better, brother. Things were getting stagnant over there. It was time for more. Haven't you ever wanted a change?"

I had. It was an answer I could relate to, and despite the fact that I knew there was more than what Cal was telling us, I dropped it. At least for the moment. "Absolutely," I agreed with him. "I'm glad you're here. Even if you are five days late."

"Four," Cal protested. "Besides, I had some things to take care of in the city. I had to stop in and see Mom."

"Mom?" Ian asked. "You saw Mom?"

"Of course. I haven't seen her in way too long." Cal laughed. "How is that even a question?" He shook his head. "No wonder I'm the favorite."

Ian punched him in the shoulder and I laughed. It was an ongoing, mostly friendly rivalry between the oldest and the youngest as to who was the favorite, and it was a battle I had learned ages ago to stay well clear of.

"Hey," Cal changed the subject. "Where's Chelsea? I couldn't believe it when Dec told me she was here. I gotta say, it's about time you guys got over yourselves and got to know the girls. They're awesome."

Another sore spot. Cal and Declan were always closer with their half-sisters. Much closer, because Ian and I had flat-out refused to get to know them when we were younger.

"They are great," I said. "Well, I'm sure Amber is. We just haven't met her yet."

"And Chelsea is…well, she's certainly a handful," Ian said. "But I'm sure you know that."

Cal laughed. "For sure. Where is she?"

"She's working."

"Working?" Cal almost spat out his beer. "Chelsea? Last I heard she was…well, Dec said she was a little lost."

I tilted my beer in Ian's direction. "A little time spent with big brother changed all that. She seems pretty focused now."

"If you can call working a regular job focused." Ian grinned. "But she is doing better. Let's go down to the Paw and say hi. Then I'll take you over to the Dockside."

"So much to catch up on." Cal laughed. "And don't forget to introduce me to your woman. I don't remember Gwen from when we were kids."

He looked to me, but I only shook my head. "Even if you did, she's a totally different person now." My eyes met Ian's before I looked back to my youngest brother. "You're going to love her."

"Of that I have no doubt," Cal said. "What about you, Mitch? I suppose you have your usual bevy of women on rotation."

"Not Mitch," Ian interjected before I could respond. "Our brother here has turned over a new leaf."

"A new leaf?"

"So it seems." Ian and Cal exchanged glances. "More of a one-woman man," Ian continued. "He just needs to find the woman."

I threw my empty beer can at Ian's head. He laughed and ducked it easily.

"Let's go." I walked back into the house and to the front door.

There was no point arguing with him, because Ian was right. I did need to find the right woman.

The problem was, I was pretty sure I already had.

Chapter Seven

JADE

IT WAS A BEAUTIFUL DAY.

Like most days at the lake, the sun was shining and even though it was still early, I could tell it was going to be another hot day. I was glad I had put on a new pair of shorts and a white linen sleeveless blouse over my bikini.

I had thought about cancelling on Mitch and his promised fun day in the sun. Even now, as I walked down Main Street toward the Dockside, I contemplated turning around and going home more than once. But what was the point? There was no reason I shouldn't have a little fun, except one very obvious one.

But it was only obvious to me.

I decided not to think about that. And not to say anything to Mitch. At least for one day. Nothing was going to change in one day, except maybe I would be able to relax and have a little fun before I had to make what could potentially be the biggest decision of my life.

Besides, nothing would be gained by telling Mitch about

the baby now. It would only ruin our day together. And more than anything, I really needed to not think about it. At least for a day.

My hand went absentmindedly to my stomach the way it had been for the last few days. It was still flat. Nobody would be able to tell. I had spent hours the day before looking in the mirror, examining myself from all sides. I could've sworn there had been a bump there the day I'd been trying on clothes. I knew now that that was stupid; there was no way I had been showing. It was probably just my subconscious mind letting me in on the secret.

So far I'd been able to push the idea of a baby out of my head, at least while I was working. In fact, losing myself in my work had been good because it gave me a chance to think about anything other than the fact that I was going to be a mom.

A mom.

That's just what I was going to do today. Lose myself in the moment. Even if it was only for a moment.

The minute I spotted Mitch on the dock, my heart leapt into my throat. I told myself it was only because he looked so damn sexy standing there next to the boat where we'd shared…well, where we had most definitely shared. But now there was another reason my body and mind were going crazy in his presence. A big reason.

No.

I wasn't going to think about it. Not today. Instead, I'd focus on how damn sexy Mitch was and try to remember why we'd decided it was best for us just to be friends.

Why had we done that again?

Right, because Mitch told me I wasn't his type and as far as I was concerned, men were nothing but trouble.

Damn, was that ever more true than it ever had been. I shook my head with the irony of it all.

Besides, Mitch was dating Evie. And Evie was a nice woman. A woman I could see myself being friends with. A woman who did not deserve to have a new relationship with a man ruined.

Besides, I didn't need a man, I reminded myself.

A man was nothing but trouble. A man would only hold me back.

Right.

They were the same things I'd repeated to myself for years. The same things my mother had drilled into my head. The same things my mother had said about having children.

I groaned. I was not doing a good job putting my troubles out of my head. Not even a little.

"Good morning, beautiful." Mitch pulled me in for a quick hug and a chaste kiss on the cheek, the same way I'd seen him greet Gwen. Like a friend. "Are you ready for this? A fun day in the sun?"

I smiled. "You've sure talked it up. Are you sure you can deliver?"

"Oh, don't worry about that." His cockiness sparked something in my gut. "I always deliver on my promises."

Heat flared in my cheeks and I had to look away.

"Well, let's get going then."

I walked toward the boat and was just about to hop in when his arm on mine stopped me. "Wait."

I froze under his touch.

"There's just one thing I need to know."

Had Deanna said something? Was my secret out already? It was a small town, after all. There was no doubt that word traveled quickly and it would be next to impossible to keep a secret like this one. I should have known better than to try to—

"Do you have sunscreen?"

"Pardon?" I turned and stared at him. "Sunscreen?"

His face was a mask of seriousness as he nodded. "It can

get pretty hot out on the water and I don't want you burning."
He trailed a finger down my bare arm. The touch sent a shiver
completely through me. "A sunburn seems like such a small
thing, but it can really ruin the fun if you're not careful."

I smiled slightly. He had no idea what kind of small thing
could ruin our fun. "Don't worry. I won't ruin any fun today." I
winked and hopped into the waiting boat.

MITCH

I HAD A GREAT DAY PLANNED. I couldn't think of anyone I'd
rather spend it with than Jade. The second she'd gotten into
the boat, she was at home. It was hard to believe that it was
only her second time on a boat ever. She was a natural.

I steered the boat away from the dock and out into the lake.
Ian hadn't been happy when he heard that not only was I
taking the whole day off, I planned on tying up some of the
rentals as well. Not that Ian had much room to complain—I
was practically working for free and I more than deserved a
day off. That being said, it was still probably a good idea to get
as far away from the Dockside as possible, as quickly as
possible.

The second we were a safe distance away from the marina,
I pressed down on the throttle and urged the boat forward.
Next to me, Jade let out a small squeal as the boat sped up.

I looked over to see her smile wide, her hair flying wildly
behind her in the wind. Nothing but joy on her face.

Sitting next to me, I could hardly believe it was the same
woman I'd met at the summer solstice festival. Sure, she was
still every bit as gorgeous—no, she was more gorgeous with the
slight bit of sun kiss on her nose and the freckles that had
appeared, softening her somehow. But she had also clearly

taken my suggestion, and gone out and gotten some lake clothes.

"I like your new look."

She turned toward me with a smile. "I'm glad you noticed. I am trying to fit in here. And I guess you are right, the dress pants and silk blouses weren't exactly lake wear." She reached over her head and tussled her hair in the wind. "I went to visit your girlfriend's new store. She's lovely."

Girlfriend? It took a minute to realize who Jade was talking about. Evelyn. I had said something about going on a date with her, not that that would make her my girlfriend. Was Jade jealous?

I scanned her, looking for signs that she might be upset. But there were none. After all, we had decided to be just friends. Maybe it was possible for a man and a woman to be just friends. Even when we clearly had such an amazing chemistry together.

At any rate, Jade seemed to be okay with it. Maybe it made her more comfortable thinking that I was seeing someone? It couldn't hurt.

"Yes. Evelyn is great. I haven't been in the shop yet, but I know she's been pretty busy with it."

"You should go. It's great. And I think I personally paid her bills for the month with all my purchases." Her laugh rang out on the air, and I had to look away.

She didn't even know how sexy she was.

I didn't want to talk about Evie anymore, but it was safer not saying anything. So I pressed down farther on the accelerator, and the boat sped forward across the lake, skimming across the water.

"Where are we going?" Jade yelled over the roar of the engine. "And are we just going to drive around all day?"

"Oh no. I promised you a day of summer fun on the lake, and that's exactly what you're going to get." I pointed to the beach we were headed straight for. "We are almost at our first destination. Are you ready for this?"

She nodded. "You have no idea."

I paused, unsure what she meant. But maybe the demands of getting a new show off the ground were proving to be more than she bargained for? It didn't matter. The only thing that mattered was that I'd promised her a great day, and I was more than ready to deliver.

I slowed the boat as we approached the shore. When I was a kid, I wouldn't have hesitated on driving right up to pull the boat up onto the beach. But I was older and wiser now. And the boat wasn't mine. It was my brother's, and I was pretty sure Ian would not hesitate to kick my ass if I dragged his new investment up on the sand and rocks.

Instead, I brought the boat to a stop, close enough to shore so that we could anchor, but deep enough that there would be no damage. I cut the engine, moved to the bow and tossed out the small anchor that would hold us in place.

"What are we doing?" Jade hopped out of her seat. "I thought we were going to have lake fun today."

I swung my arms out around me. "This is the lake," I said. "And I promise we are going to have fun."

"But we're not moving." Gingerly, Jade walked through the boat toward me. "And it's fun when we're moving." She smiled and stopped walking; the boat rocked a little so she held onto the windshield.

Damn, she looked so at ease on the boat. So natural. How could I have ever thought she was a city girl? She'd only been in town a month or so, but clearly it agreed with her.

"I promise this will be fun too."

She stuck her bottom lip out in a pretend pout. I had to hold myself back from closing the distance between us, pulling her into my arms, and kissing that pout right off her face.

Instead, I fiddled with the rope. I wrapped it around the cleat on the side of the boat to secure the anchor.

"Okay," she said, but I could tell she wasn't entirely convinced. "I trust you. So what are we doing here?"

I straightened up and pointed to the beach where I had stashed some supplies earlier in the morning. "We're going to shore."

"That doesn't seem like the lake."

"I thought you said you trusted me? We just need to go to shore to pick up a new boat." I pointed at the paddleboards lying on the sand and pulled my T-shirt over my head before I tossed it onto the seat beside me. "Are you ready?"

"Paddleboards?" I could see she was trying not to look, but I caught the way her eyes tracked over my bare chest. Her gaze made my cock twitch. "I've never tried a paddleboard. And besides that, how exactly are we getting to shore?"

"First," I grinned, "if you've never tried paddleboarding, you don't know what you're missing. It's the very definition of lake fun. And second...please tell me you know how to swim. Because this day will be very different if you can't." I hadn't even considered the fact that she might not know how to swim. I just took it for granted that if you were at the lake, you knew how to swim.

"Of course I know how to swim." She crossed her arms over her chest, not in any way looking like even if she could, that she actually did want to swim.

"Then what's the holdup? Don't tell me you're afraid of getting wet. I mean, we wouldn't want to ruin your hair," I teased.

My teasing had the desired effect, just as I knew it would. Jade straightened her shoulders. And narrowed her eyes in challenge. "Do I look like that kind of girl?"

A few weeks ago, I would've said yes. But now, there was something different about Jade. It was just slight. Fundamentally, she was the same person. But her edge had softened a little, and I liked it.

Jade didn't wait for an answer. Her fingers moved to her blouse and started undoing the buttons there. I had to look away, or risk what could be an embarrassing and uncomfortable situation in my shorts. Instead of watching her, I stood on the seat at the bow of the boat and looked down into the water. It was deep enough to dive.

"What are you waiting for?" Jade moved until she stood next to me. The boat dipped with our combined weight on the bench. She smelled of coconut sun lotion, mixed with her familiar spicy scent.

"I was just making sure you wouldn't chicken out."

"I don't chicken out." She stretched her arms over her head, and I got an eyeful of her creamy white skin and an impossibly small bikini. I'd seen her naked, but somehow seeing her with the red scraps of fabric just barely covering her breasts, the string tied in a knot on her back—not to mention the triangle that stretched over her perfect ass—it was the most erotic thing I'd ever seen.

I sucked in a breath, hoping she hadn't noticed the effect she had on me.

"I can see that."

Jade tipped her head with a wicked smile in my direction. "Last one to the beach is a rotten egg." Before I could even respond, she had pointed her arms over her head, and with a smooth dive, arced gracefully into the water.

Oh no, she didn't.

There was no way I was going to let her beat me. Not like that. With a much less graceful dive, I followed her into the water and gave chase.

Chapter Eight

JADE

NOT ONLY COULD I SWIM, I'd been on my school swim team growing up. Mitch might have size and strength on his side, but he was no match for my speed. Despite the fact that it had been years since I'd been in the water, I beat him easily and stood on the shore with my hands on my hips when he finally joined me. "Took you long enough."

He stood bent over, hands on his knees, sucking in air. When he finally caught his breath, he looked up and shook his head with a laugh. "I should've known. Let me guess, swim club?"

"Captain." I turned, and with a wiggle in my hips, walked toward the paddleboards. I hadn't been lying when I said I had never been on a paddleboard, and I was a little nervous, but I was excited too. Spending time with Mitch was easy and fun, and if he suggested it, I knew it would be good.

Recovered from his swim, Mitch joined me walking along the sand toward the paddleboards. "Don't tell me," he said. "You really are a pro paddleboarder too."

He reached down and grabbed two paddles, handing me one.

"No," I said. "I really have never tried it. I assume you'll teach me."

He straightened up and puffed his chest out with pride. "Baby, I'll show you everything you need to know. Let me get the boards ready."

I waited while he dragged the boards down to the water, flipped them over and made them ready. He waved me over and gave me basic instructions on how to kneel on the board before standing up. He made it look easy. Of course, he'd been doing it for years. But how hard could it be?

Doing as instructed, I laid the paddle across the board and climbed up. It wiggled underneath me and I paused to regain my balance. As soon as I felt stable, I put my right foot up, followed by my left, and stood. I felt the board move to the left, as my body moved to the right, and the next thing I knew, I was surfacing in the lake while my board floated away.

I wiped the hair from my eyes and smoothed it back over my head, processing what had just happened.

It had seemed so simple. How could that have gone wrong?

His laughter registered in my brain, and I spun around in the water to look for him.

Spotting him, I narrowed my eyes in a glare. He stood proud on his board, not even bothering to hide his amusement.

I had to admit, it was pretty funny. But that didn't mean I wasn't going to make him pay. Before he could spot me, I dove under the water and kicked hard in his direction. I surfaced next to his board, startling him.

"Hey," he said, barely able to speak through his laughter. "What are you doing in there?"

"Pretty funny, huh?"

He nodded.

With a hard kick, I propelled myself upward and reached

for the opposite side of his board. I grabbed hold and yanked it toward me, flipping his paddleboard out from under him.

With a satisfying splash, he landed somewhere behind me. He surfaced, sputtering and still laughing. "That's it," he said. "I'm going to get you."

A thrill raced through me. "You'll have to catch me first."

"Baby, I only let you win before." He wiped the water from his face and grinned. "But now, you're mine."

It might have been the fact that he was giving chase or it could have been his choice of words, but my heart raced and I let out a squeal, before I dove under the water to put the board between us. When I resurfaced, he was gone.

I scanned the water's surface, but it was perfectly calm. Not even a ripple. My heart beat faster with anticipation. I kicked hard and spun myself around and then he was there. Inches from me.

"Gotcha."

"How did you—"

My words were lost as he grabbed my bare arms and pulled me close, pressing his chest against mine. The water was cold but with his skin on mine, there was nothing but heat between us. "I have my ways." His words were punctuated by puffs of air on my lips, he was so close.

I could've kissed him. Maybe I should have kissed him. But it would only do more harm than good. Besides, friends didn't kiss. But I needed to get away from him because his proximity was testing me. And it didn't feel like a test I could pass.

I held my breath and slipped out of his hands under the water. With a strong kick, I propelled myself toward the board that was only a few feet away.

I grabbed onto the board, and with a big kick, hopped on top. "Okay, now that I know what I'm dealing with, let's do this."

"You might need a paddle." He laughed and swam easily toward the paddles floating a short distance away.

I waited until he handed me one before I repeated the steps to stand up. This time I knew what to expect; I rose to my feet with only a little bit of wobbling.

"See? I can do it."

Next to me, he was already standing on his board, looking as if he'd spent all his days standing on the wobbly surface. It would've been annoying how good he was at things, if he didn't look so damn sexy doing them.

"Maybe if my teacher had given me the proper instruction in the first place," I grinned, "I'd already be paddling circles around you. I know your game—just trying to keep me down."

With strong, sure strokes, he paddled toward me. "Oh baby, if I was trying to keep you down, there'd only be one reason for it."

"That how you talk to a friend these days?" I dipped my paddle in the water and with a heave, splashed water over him. "Maybe that'll cool you off."

He laughed. I was no fool. I knew what I'd started and I wasn't about to stick around to see what he would do in retaliation. Bracing my legs, I dug the paddle into the lake and pulled back, propelling myself forward. It was so smooth, so much easier than I thought it would be. I'd seen paddleboarding on TV before and always thought it looked so calm and smooth. Maybe it would be, if he wasn't giving chase. A laugh bubbled from my throat, as I forced myself to paddle faster and not fall over.

"You know, I could tip you if I wanted to."

I looked to my left. There he was, traveling on his board right next to me, only an arm's length away.

"But you don't want to?"

"I want to do a lot of things, Jade."

Water droplets dripped off his hard, muscular chest. I tried not to stare. No, I tried not to lick my lips. Because I had never been drawn to a man the way I was with him. Why did things have to be so complicated? It didn't matter. I shook my head and refocused. He was with Evie now.

"But what I want most of all," he continued, "is to have a great day with you. And there's something I want to show you. Are you up for it?"

I nodded. There was nothing I'd rather be doing than spending the day with Mitch.

"Great. Have you ever seen an eagle's nest before?" I shook my head, not that I needed to. He would've known the answer to that question. "It's the coolest thing," he said. "And you can only get to it by water. I wanted to take you by paddleboard because it's quieter, and maybe we'll actually get to see one of the babies. The engine from the boat scares the mother."

Together we paddled side by side, the conversation easy and light as we made our way along the water's edge. He was right. The eagle's nest was the coolest thing I had ever seen. Living in the city, I never realized how much I missed out on. It was remarkable.

We weren't able to see the babies from where we were floating on our boards, but just to see an eagle so close up, the mother keeping watch on the edge of the nest, was incredible.

We didn't speak much as we made our way back to the beach. But it was an easy silence. I had never experienced such an ease with a man before. Maybe it was because we decided just to be friends. Maybe it was because we had taken sex out of the equation.

Whatever it was, I didn't want to lose it. My thoughts drifted momentarily to the secret I still kept. Once he knew, everything would change. And I needed to be ready for that.

MITCH

THE FLICKERS and flames of the campfire mesmerized me. I stared into the coals momentarily before I tossed another log on to the fire. It had been a great day. Probably one of the best in recent memory. Hell, I couldn't remember having so much fun with Bethany. For a while, I'd even considered marrying her. That seemed like a million years ago now.

"What are you thinking about?"

We'd been sitting in silence for a few minutes. It had been an easy silence. With no pressure to talk about mundane things. Things that just didn't matter. But I liked talking to Jade, and I welcomed the question.

"Honestly?" Normally I would never think of telling a woman what I was about to. But she just seemed different. She nodded, so I continued. "I was just thinking about how glad I am, that I met you." In the dancing firelight, I saw something flicker across her face. But it may have just been the flames, so I continued. "And how glad I am that I knew when to get out and come back to the lake."

Jade sat up and wrapped the blanket tighter around her shoulders. "Get out of where?"

"Out of the future that would've been bad for me." There was no point going into details, especially because the more I lived in the now, the more I realized I was in the right place.

Maybe even with the right person.

It wasn't a new thought, and it wasn't one that surprised me. Ironically, it was probably the date with Evie that concreted things for me. I had been so busy focusing on what I thought I should want, I hadn't even seen what I needed. I was more and more sure that what I needed was Jade.

Maybe I just needed to convince her.

"I think finally, after so many years of trying something else, I'm finally back where I should be. At the lake. Something about this place fills your soul. Do you agree? Or do you think I'm crazy?"

Across from me, Jade nodded. "While I do think you're crazy." She laughed before she continued. "I also agree with you. As you know, I've never spent any time at a lake before."

"I still think that's a terrible shame."

She smiled in agreement. "I only planned on spending the summer here. Just long enough to get things going with the show. After all, I'm a city girl. That's all I've ever been. It's all I know, really."

She stared into the fire, but I knew there was more. "And now? How do you feel now?"

She didn't answer the question right away, but I didn't rush her. "Do you know when you've always been told one thing, and you've been told that thing so many times, that it is the only thing you believe to be true?"

It wasn't really a question, but I nodded in agreement anyway.

"My mother was a single mom," Jade continued. "I never knew my father. Except for what my mom told me. That he'd ruined her life." I opened my mouth to object, but Jade shook her head so I stayed silent. "I don't think she meant me necessarily. It was everything all together. You see, she was on track to be a successful businesswoman. When she met my dad, she was working for an oil and gas company. She was focused and determined. She had goals and plans. She had been working her way up in the company, taking on more and more accounts. It was her dream to be an executive one day. She used to tell me she wasn't like other girls who always dreamed about getting married and having a family. But then she met my dad."

"And then she fell in love?"

Jade nodded and her lips quirked up into a small smile. "I always thought it would've been cool to see her like that. Young and in love. Because no matter what she said, there must've been a time when everything was good and right with her world."

"Of course," I agreed. "Love is a good thing, isn't it?" I wasn't really sure, but even to my own ears it sounded like a loaded question. If Jade noticed, she didn't say anything.

"I think it was," she said. "At least for a little while. The way she tells it, she got distracted and her work started to suffer. She started losing accounts because instead of working all the time, she was with him. She said she didn't care, because she was in love and that was all that mattered. And then she got pregnant."

The dancing flames cast a momentary shadow on Jade's face. And then it was gone.

"I don't really know what happened from there—she never really goes into details. All I know is that he left, I was born, and her career crashed."

"But it's not your fault."

Jade shook her head. "No. And honestly, she never made me feel like it was my fault. But she did make sure that I knew a man would never be worth it."

I shook my head and poked the fire with a stick. "That's heavy."

Jade shrugged and dropped the blanket to the ground behind her. "It is what it is." She stretched her lean arms over her head, her bare skin glowing both from the firelight and the result of being kissed by the sun. She was always beautiful. But after a day in the sun, her hair air dried in gentle waves around her face, and not a trace of makeup on her, she was the most stunning creature I had ever seen.

I had a feeling I wasn't going to like the answers if I asked any more questions, but I couldn't seem to help myself. Despite everything I'd been telling myself and trying to convince myself of since coming back to Cedar Springs, I was starting to think the impossible had actually started to happen and I was falling for Jade. And that both scared the hell out of me while at the same time, it felt very, very right.

"And what do you think?" The question was out of my mouth before I'd thought it through. "Do you think a man is worth it?"

Jade shrugged and trailed her fingers through the sand next to her. "Honestly?"

"Of course."

"I guess on some level I've always kind of agreed with her." My heart sank. "But I've never actually given it that much thought. My mom was always so busy encouraging me to be successful, and work hard, and achieve my dreams. Those things never went hand-in-hand with a man, or relationship of any kind." Jade sat up abruptly. The sand slid through her fingers. "But I don't want to give you the impression that she is a terrible woman. She's not. She's just... Focused."

"And it sounds like she passed that on to you. You've been very successful in your career."

Jade nodded. "I have. I've achieved almost everything I want to. At least at this point. That's why I took on this TV project. It's not normally something that I would even consider." Jade gazed into the fire and her eyes took on a faraway look. "I think I'm just ready for new challenges. Maybe I'm starting to realize that my mom wasn't totally right."

I almost missed the last part of what she said. Almost. "What part do you think she was wrong about?"

Her smile was coy, but also guarded. "Let's just say that being in Cedar Springs is teaching me that there's more to life than a career and maybe I'm finally ready to start exploring another side of things."

I watched the reflection of the flames dance on Jade's bare skin. I yearned to be sitting close enough to touch her. But despite the closeness we'd shared all day, there was also still something between us. Something keeping us apart.

Could it be that I said she wasn't my type? My inner voice piped up.

For sure, I was to blame in a large part for whatever it was creating distance between us. I'd been stupid, that was for sure. What kind of ridiculousness was it to think that I needed to have a certain type of woman in order to be happy? When it was so clear, the only type of woman I needed was the one who made me happy.

And God help me, I was pretty sure that woman was Jade.

Chapter Nine

JADE

I WAS RUNNING LATE. I never ran late. I could come up with a million excuses for why I'd slept through my alarm. And given half a chance, I could come up with a list of things that kept me from falling asleep last night, and therefore caused me to sleep in. I could do all of those things. But I wouldn't, because they would just be excuses. And I hated excuses.

The truth was I was running late for my meeting with Gwen because even when my alarm went off this morning, I had somehow convinced myself it was just a dream in order to buy myself a few more minutes. It had worked, too, except now I was going to be late.

The day before, spending all day with Mitch on the lake—playing in the sun, laughing, forgetting about everything else in my life—had been amazing. But it had also been exhausting.

That might be the hormones, too.

I ignored my inner voice, which suddenly seemed to be a pregnancy expert. Sure, I could be exhausted because I was pregnant and in my first trimester. Deanna had said something about needing more rest during these months. But I wasn't going to let a baby slow me down. No, I was tired because I'd spent the day before out in the sun, playing in the water, and I'd gotten home late.

But it had been worth it.

Just thinking about my day with Mitch caused me to slow down and reflect on how much fun I'd had. Was it even possible to have a platonic relationship with a man? Maybe it was. If yesterday was any indication, then yes, we could be friends.

Except for the amazingly intense attraction I had toward him. Oh, and the little fact that I was carrying his baby.

I shook my head and sighed so loud it caught the attention of a passerby, who gave me a strange look and a wide berth. Even after getting home last night, late and exhausted, I still couldn't sleep. There were so many questions going through my head. So much second-guessing.

Should I have told him? I probably should have. But was it so wrong to want one day of fun, stress-free? Because I wasn't stupid. The minute I told him about the baby, everything was going to change. Especially if I decided to keep it and raise it as a single mom.

That particular thought had been making an appearance in my brain more and more often. I worked so hard to develop a reputation as a strong, no-nonsense business woman with no time for anything but work, the idea that I even was considering keeping the baby was ludicrous to me.

Was it?

Regardless, I was going to have to make a decision about how and when to tell Mitch the truth. And soon. It wasn't fair to keep it from him, especially if he was starting a new relationship with Evie. They both deserved to know.

I sighed one more time, straightened my shoulders, smoothed my hands over my hair and patted the quick bun I tied it back in that morning, and opened the door to Dream Puffs, ready for my meeting.

Across the room, Gwen stood and waved excitedly when she saw me. "Over here. I got your coffee."

Coffee.

Deanna hadn't outright said it was bad for the baby, but she had given me a pamphlet with a list of some of the things I should avoid or cut down on. I waved in Gwen's direction and with a series of hand gestures I hoped the other woman understood, I made my way up to the counter to order myself a tea.

"Coffee?" Suzy greeted me warmly like a regular, which maybe I was by now. "I think Gwen got one for you. Black. Just the way you like it." The fact that this woman knew how I took my coffee made me smile. Had anyone ever known how I took my coffee? I was pretty sure my mother might have been the only one who'd bothered to notice and that's only because I drank it the same way she did.

"Actually, I think I'm going to have a tea today," I said apologetically. "If it's not too much trouble."

"None at all. What would you like? We have peppermint, black, Earl Grey, green, apple cinnamon, chamomile, jasmine—"

"Peppermint will be fine." I interrupted her because she sounded like she might only just be getting started. "Thanks, Suzy."

The older woman went to prepare my drink, and I turned at the sound of the bells over the door just in time to see Evie walk in. My initial reaction to seeing the woman I'd only recently come to know was a flicker of jealousy, but I swallowed it. Evie was way too nice to be jealous over.

"Jade!" Evie greeted me with a warm smile. "You look amazing. I like your outfit." She winked and I couldn't help but laugh.

"Thank you." I spun dramatically to show off my floral

print blouse and tan capris. It was casual yet still business and I felt fantastic in it. "I know this great little spot with the prettiest clothes and the sweetest shop keeper to help you find just the right thing."

Evie squealed with a delight and pulled me into a quick hug. It took me off guard. I was not usually a hugger, so it took me a minute to loosen up and hug the woman back. But it was brief and left me feeling strange. Not necessarily in a bad way, but it felt wrong to have almost kissed the man this woman was dating, less than twenty-four hours before. Like a betrayal to our blooming friendship.

"How are things with Mitch?" I looked away as I asked the question, unable to look the other woman in the face. "I hope he wasn't too upset that I made you late for your date the other night. If I had realized, I wouldn't have come in so late."

When Evie didn't answer right away, I looked up to see puzzlement on her face. "Mitch?" She gave me an unsure smile. "What do you mean, how are things? We're just friends. I mean, we did go on one date, but...well, maybe I should have made it more clear. Did he say something?"

"I'm sorry," I said quickly. "I didn't realize. I think I just... well, I think I just assumed," I admitted, feeling foolish as I did so. Why had I assumed they were a couple? It was ridiculous, really. Mitch hadn't mentioned her the day before and besides knowing they'd gone out...well, it certainly didn't add up to a relationship.

"It's fine," Evie said, clearly not nearly as bothered by the assumption as I was. "I think Mitch is a great guy, and what he did for my son...well, I don't think I'll ever be able to repay him." Her pretty face twisted into worry. "He doesn't think that we're—"

"Oh no," I said quickly. "I mean, he didn't say anything to me, anyway. I just assumed." I swallowed hard and tried for a smile. "Sorry. I really put my foot in it."

Evie squeezed my arm. "Please don't worry about it. It's all good." Suzy returned with the tea, offering me a welcomed distraction from my awkwardness. But it only lasted as long as it took me to pay, and then Evie said, "You know...this is going to sound crazy, but you and Mitch seem like you'd be a good match."

"That is crazy." I forced a laugh and shook my head.

"Is it?" Evie examined me far too closely, as if she could see my secret. "I don't know," she continued. "I think you guys could be perfect for each other."

"Well, that's maybe a thought for another day." I did my best to brush it off, and fortunately was saved by the sound of the bells over the door once more. "But it looks like it's time to get to work." I pointed to the man who'd just walked in. Judging by the look on Evie's face when she turned to see Cal McCormick, looking every bit the movie star with his aviator sunglasses, faded jeans, and slightly too tight T-shirt, walk into the bakery, no introduction was necessary.

The other woman had turned an intense shade of pink. "Is that..."

"Cal McCormick?" I grinned just as Gwen called out to him. "Sure is," I finished. "He's in town to film the show. Don't tell me you have a crush on him?"

Evie laughed and her color returned to normal. "No way. I mean, he's cute and all but celebrities are not my type. Not even a little. Single moms don't have that kind of luxury. When I finally decide to date again, it will be with a down-to-earth, regular guy. No flash. Just a normal, stable guy." I raised my cup to my new friend's ideals. "But he is pretty cute," Evie added as we watched him cross the room.

I nodded in agreement. There was definitely a family resemblance, and Cal was good-looking, that was certain. But he wasn't as sexy as Mitch. Not even close. "I'm sure having him around for the summer could make it interesting for a lot of women in town."

Evie nudged me and pointed to a table by the window where a pretty girl sat. She was trying to be subtle about the way she was watching Cal, but as far as I was concerned, she wasn't doing a very good job. "I think someone might have a little crush already."

I laughed and shook my head. "It will be interesting to see, for sure. But I'm already running late, so I better get going."

"Of course," Evie said. "Me too. We'll have to meet for a coffee soon when we can both sit and chat."

"I'd like that," I answered honestly.

"Oh, and Jade? I was telling you the truth when I said I'm not dating Mitch McCormick." Her grin was sly. "So, he's totally available for you."

It was my turn to blush, but I didn't answer as I walked quickly to the table to make my meeting.

MITCH

"I THINK you will really like this property," Milena Hill said as she walked next to me down the street away from the cabin. "It was only listed a few days ago. I haven't even had the chance to show it to anyone. But when you emailed me your list of requirements and what you're looking for—well, there is nothing else that checks all your boxes like this property."

I grinned at her enthusiasm. There was nothing I liked less than house shopping. I bought my place in the city after only looking at two places. It was easier to sign the paperwork than to put myself through the process any longer.

"I hope so," I said. "And thank you for showing me something so quickly. I hope you at least had time to have breakfast." It was early but Milena had shown up right away, dressed and ready to work. Her outfit reminded me a lot of Jade's new clothes. I liked Jade's new look—not that she didn't look amazing before—but now she looked as if she not only belonged at the lake but might actually stay.

The idea gave me pause. But only because I wanted her to stay in Cedar Springs more than I wanted anything else at that moment.

After spending the day with her, I couldn't sleep. I should have been exhausted after a whole day in the sun and on the water, but all I could think about was the way the firelight danced off her skin, the spicy, sexy smell of her when I hugged her good night. I may not have wanted it, but it was happening. No, scratch that. It had happened. I'd fallen in love with Jade.

When the sun finally came up, the decision had already been made. I made myself a pot of coffee and called Declan. Regardless of the time change, I knew my little brother would be up, whatever time. Declan was always awake. Sure enough, my little brother answered on the second ring.

"Hey. Long time no talk." Declan's voice came across the line. It always amazed me how my brother could be a world away, and still sound as if he were in the same room.

"I know, sorry."

"It's not a problem," Dec said. "I know you've been busy. It's all good. How's the lake?"

"Damn, Dec. I forgot how much I love it here. In fact, that's why I'm calling. Besides, of course, talking to my favorite brother."

Declan laughed. "It seems I'm everybody's favorite—when you guys want something, of course. What can I do for you?"

The idea had been percolating all night. In the light of day, I had wondered whether it would look any different. But the only thing that was different was instead of it just being an idea, I was ready to make it a reality. "I need to buy a house."

"A house? In the city? I thought you had a house."

"I do. But I want one here. At the lake."

Dec was quiet for a moment. "What's wrong with the cabin? Please don't tell me you're fighting with our brother. Or…it's not Chelsea, is it?"

"Oh, God no. Chelsea is great. And I hate to admit it, but you were right all these years. We should have gotten to know her sooner."

"No," Dec said. "It wasn't time then. I don't think it would be the same. But I'm glad it's happening now." I was glad too. "So if it's not Chelsea…what the hell happened?"

I laughed. "It's not Ian," I said. "You don't have to assume the worst, Dec. It's nothing but happy sibling harmony over here. In fact, Cal just showed up."

"Cal is there too?"

I thought I could detect a bit of envy in my brother's voice.

"He is. And that's kind of the problem. I know the house seemed plenty big when we were kids. But as you can imagine, it gets a whole lot smaller now that we're all grown up. And don't forget that Ian has Gwen living in the house too. It's cozy. To say the least."

"Of course—that is a full house. So, if you're looking to buy, you're looking for a cabin?"

It was an option, of course. I did have a house in the city. Hell, my job was in the city. But when I thought about buying property in Cedar Springs, it wasn't just a summer home I was after. It was a permanent place. I would figure the job thing out later. "No," I said. "I'm ready to move. Who do you know in town who could help me out?"

That had been two hours ago, and already I was headed to see my first property with Milena Hill, the name Declan had given me. I had sent an email right away, not expecting a reply for a few hours at the very least. To my surprise, Milena responded right away. She was fairly newly licensed and eager to help out. And according to her response, she had the perfect place for me.

"One of the best parts about this place is how close it is to your family home," Milena said now. She smiled, and for the first time, I noticed how pretty she was. She was soft, with a spattering of freckles across her nose. A very girl-next-door type. And from what I could tell, she was a lovely lady. Maybe even a nice girl. A month ago—hell, a few weeks ago—I might have even asked her out.

But now the only woman I could think about was Jade. And if I was honest, she'd been the only woman all along. The fact that I was now firmly in the friend zone was something I'd figure out shortly. But first, the house.

"That will be a bonus for sure," I said. "And really, I do want to thank you for taking the time to help me out on such short notice today."

"It's no problem, really. I owe Declan for referring me. It was really nice of him, and when you're new in the business like I am, you can use all the referrals you can get."

"How do you know Declan?" On one hand, I knew my brother had connections everywhere. The brothers all joked about it, because Dec really was the nicest guy they knew. Seemed as if he knew everyone, and not only did everyone know him, they loved him.

"It's crazy, really," she said. "We kind of knew each other when we were kids. But it's not like we were friends or anything. And then one day I saw him and his organization on social media. I thought he looked familiar and commented on one of his posts. He replied right away, and he remembered me. After that, I guess, we just became friends." She held the clipboard tightly to her ample chest and smiled. "I know you can say what you want to about social media, but it really does connect people."

I nodded. I couldn't disagree with that. "Well, I'm sure glad you guys were able to reconnect, especially if it means you have the perfect house to sell me today." We laughed and for the next few minutes fell into easy conversation, until Milena stopped walking and pointed up the drive at what was in fact, the perfect house.

Chapter Ten

JADE

"THAT WENT REALLY WELL, don't you think?" Gwen turned to me, but I still stared at Cal across the table. He'd just finished reading lines as an informal audition to play his brother. I nodded absently in Gwen's direction, but I couldn't stop staring at Cal.

He was perfect. Maybe it was because he was a great actor just waiting to be discovered. Maybe it was because he was so similar to his brother in so many ways that it was easy to embody the character. Whatever it was, it didn't matter because for the first time in a few weeks, I felt really excited about the project. Not that I hadn't been excited before but it had been easy to lose sight of the joy once I'd gotten bogged down with all the details. But now that I was confident we had the right actor to play Ian, it was once again starting to feel real.

"Jade?"

I snapped out of my private thoughts and looked to both Gwen and Cal, who watched me, waiting for my response.

I focused on Gwen for a moment. She looked as if she was about to bounce out of her seat. Clearly she felt the reading had gone just as well as I did.

I shifted my glance to Cal, who actually looked nervous. I hadn't expected that. After all, he was a professional.

I kept my face a careful mask of neutrality for another moment longer.

"Jade!"

I couldn't keep it up. I let myself smile. "I think we've found our Ian McCormick."

Cal let out a whoop and his face split into a smile. It was clear to see how he so successfully made his living. The man was gorgeous.

"Seriously?" Gwen grabbed my arm. "You think so, too?"

"Of course." I nodded. "He was great. So natural and, you were the perfect mix of sexy and humble. It was perfect. I think you're just the Ian McCormick we're looking for."

Cal laughed. "I can't tell you how strange that sounds."

"Tell me about it," Gwen said. "That's my fiancé you're talking about." She shook her head. "But it's crazy how similar you guys are. I think you're going to be perfect." Gwen jumped up and hugged her soon-to-be brother-in-law before running around the table and giving me a spontaneous hug as well. "This is all coming together."

Was it? I wasn't quite as confident as Gwen. The script Cal had just read from wasn't really a script at all, but some rough scribblings Gwen had pulled together the night before and not only was that concerning, it was borderline panic-inducing. I had promised Peter I'd have a script in hand and it would be perfect, but that had yet to materialize.

"It's starting to," I said cautiously. "We still have a few more details to work out, of course."

"Of course." Cal leaned in, his arms on the table. "Who's

going to play Gwen? Do you have an actress picked out or will you be holding auditions?"

"I'd like Clara Lively, of course."

I stared at Gwen. "Clara Lively? As in Hollywood's biggest star, Clara Lively?"

She nodded, completely serious. "I don't think that will happen." There was no way Clara Lively was going to drop her Hollywood lifestyle to come to Cedar Springs and work on a completely unknown show. I told Gwen as much. "No offense, Cal," I added. "I mean, you're definitely an up-and-comer, but this is still a completely new show with a risky concept and we're being given a lot of free rein here, but I don't—"

"So no?"

Gwen shook her head. "I don't think so."

"Any ideas then?" Cal asked again.

I had received a call from Peter that he had some ideas for who should play the lead, including an actress who was flying into LA for the audition, but I hadn't found a chance yet to reply so I simply said, "We have a few leads, but nothing for sure. Can I have the office forward your agent a contract then? Is this official?" I shifted the subject.

Cal clapped his hands. "Absolutely."

"Excellent. We should celebrate," Gwen declared. "I know it's not even noon, but we should have a toast to celebrate. We should go to the Paw for some champagne. I'll call Ian and he can meet us there."

"Why not?" I was caught up in the moment, but I still needed to have a chat with Gwen about the script, or it would be my ass on the line. "Cal, would you mind going ahead? I need to talk a few things over with Gwen before we join you."

"Nothing serious, I hope?"

"Not at all." I smiled and kept it light until he left us alone.

Then I turned to my friend. "What's going on, Gwen? You told me you'd have a script and—"

"I know. I know. It's just that it's…well, it's different than posting on socials."

"Of course it is. But you wrote those lines that Cal just read and they were great."

"You think so?"

"Um, yes." Was Gwen really having self-confidence issues? She was one of the most self-confident women I had ever met. She had completely transformed her life and singlehandedly created a social media empire that was the entire reason we were sitting there at that moment. Was she having performance anxiety? "Gwen, it was fantastic." I reached for her hand. "Are you really questioning your own capability on this project? You have no reason to be nervous, Gwen. You're writing about your life."

"That's the hard part." She dropped her head between her hands and leaned on the table. "It's so strange to think that people are going to be watching my life play out on TV. Don't you think that's weird?"

I hadn't really stopped to think about it but I could see how it might be a little bit strange for sure. But I wasn't going to tell Gwen that. "It's going to be awesome," I said. "You're going to be awesome. But you really do need to start writing it. Peter wants to see something, but he's given me the authority to approve it. Does that help? At least a little?"

Gwen nodded. "It actually does. Will you read what I have?"

I forced myself not to clap. I'd assumed Gwen didn't have anything written at all. The fact that she had something, anything at all, was not only the best thing I'd heard all day, but possibly all week. "Of course." I forced myself to be calm. "In fact, if you could send it over later today I'll get started right away. I'm sure it's amazing. And now that you have one of the main actors, doesn't that help?"

Gwen nodded again. "It really does. Do we really have a lead actress who's interested as well?"

"I think so." I shrugged. "The LA office is handling most of the casting but Peter wanted me to be involved in the main roles. Did you want to know more?"

"Oh, God no." Gwen shook her head so violently I almost laughed. "I mean, don't get me wrong. I do like having some say in it, but I'm happy to let you and the rest of the professionals handle the heavy lifting."

"I'd hardly call myself a television professional. But it is kind of fun being involved," I agreed. "What do you say we get going and go celebrate? And then you can—" My stomach twisted so violently, I clasped a hand over my mouth, afraid I was going to be sick.

"Jade." Gwen was out of her chair and next to me in an instant. "Are you okay? You look green."

With my hand still clasped over my mouth, I nodded slightly. I inhaled deeply through my nose and let the breath out slowly. A moment later, the nausea passed and I straightened my shoulders before tentatively dropping my hand. "I think I'm okay now."

Gwen eyed me strangely. "Are you sure?"

I took another breath. This one a little deeper. "I…I think so. Yes. I'm not sure what just happened." But I knew. It had happened before and was happening more and more frequently, mostly at inconvenient times. Not at all in the morning the way I'd assumed it would.

Judging by the look that had just come over Gwen's face, she, too, knew what was going on. Her smile grew wide and she started to flap her hand as if she would burst.

"No," I said, quickly shutting her down. "Don't even think that."

"Think what?" Gwen fluttered her hands to her chest and mimed a horrified expression. "I mean, if I didn't know better, I would think that you might be—"

"Don't say it!"

Gwen must have seen something in my eyes, because the smile faded, although not disappearing altogether, and she resumed her seat next to me. "Say what?" Her eyes danced mischievously. "That you're—"

"I told you not to say it."

"But…are you?"

I really wanted to just tell Gwen the truth, but I couldn't. Not yet. I shook my head. "No. Of course not. And I don't need there to be any rumors or anything getting back to Mitch."

"Mitch?" Gwen all but yelled the name out in the bakery.

I jumped up and grabbed her hand before I sat down again. Hard. "I told you. I don't want any rumors started." My eyes drilled into my friend's, forcing her to understand. A look of hurt crossed Gwen's face, and I tried not to feel guilty. "Besides, there's nothing to tell him."

Tell him.

There was *so* much to tell him. And I'd do that. Soon.

The nausea returned, this time for an entirely different reason.

———

MITCH

"WELL, I think we should celebrate, don't you?"

"Absolutely." I was more than ready to celebrate the purchase of my new home. I couldn't even believe it happened so quickly. Anytime any kind of deal like that went smoothly, it was definitely reason to celebrate. Although, the celebrating I'd like to do involved a certain feisty brunette. But that would have to wait.

Would she be excited to find out I was moving to Cedar Springs? It was hard to tell with Jade. She had definitely implied she was looking for change herself, and with the show, she was going to be sticking around for a while. Maybe I'd be able to convince her to stick around for a whole lot longer.

"The best place I can think of to do that is the Grizzly Paw," Milena said. "Are you up for it?"

It was barely past noon, but I was definitely up for it. It only took us a few minutes to walk from Milena's real estate office on Main Street to the Paw. I held the door open for her and together we walked in to the bar.

Just as I'd expected, the place was already starting to fill up the way it always did on a summer day. It brought a smile to my face to see how well local businesses were doing in Cedar Springs. Although, it did provide more of a challenge for the locals to find a table, but we were up to the task. And as it turned out, we didn't even have to look long because the moment she spotted us, Gwen stood up and waved us over. My heart leapt and something low in my gut tightened when I saw who she was sitting with.

Jade.

Had it really only been a day since I'd seen her? Not even —only a few hours really. But still my pulse quickened at the sight of her.

"What do you think?" I asked Milena. "Are you up for joining them?" I glanced at the woman next to me, and even in the dim light I could see the blush on her cheeks. When I followed her gaze, I could see it landed squarely on my little brother, who was walking back to their table from the bar.

No way. Not that it surprised me, really. Ladies always seem to have a bit of a crush on Cal, especially those who knew who he was. Something about being a famous model had women lining up for him.

"Have you met my brother?" I asked her when she hadn't answered my first question.

She shook her head in response. "Not really," she said. "I mean, when we were kids, I knew who he was and…"

"Well then, this seems like the perfect opportunity for a proper introduction."

I greeted Gwen with a quick hug and my brother with a slap on the back, but I hesitated when I greeted Jade. What I wanted to do was grab her and give her a kiss on the lips. The kind of kiss that was definitely not suitable for a public place. The kind of kiss that was absolutely not appropriate, considering we were just friends. The kind of kiss that would let her know exactly what I wanted.

I settled for a quick hug and snuck in a chaste kiss on the cheek at the last minute. "It's nice to see you again." It was a stupid thing to say, but it was the only thing I could think of that was halfway appropriate. Especially considering she had no clue how drastically my feelings had changed. Or more accurately, how I'd finally accepted my true feelings.

"Cal, have you met Milena Hill? She's just been helping me out this morning with something very important." I didn't miss the little look Jade gave Milena out of the side of her eye. Was she jealous? Or maybe she knew what Milena did for a living and had already guessed what we had been up to? Oh, I was going to enjoy telling her.

With all of his usual charisma, Cal took Milena's hand, gave her a deadly smile, and kissed the top of it slowly. "Did we know each other when we were kids? That seems like a million years ago," he said. "It is very nice to meet you, Milena."

"Milena," Gwen said, distracting her from Cal's gaze. "I'm so glad to see you again." She glanced at Jade and said as a way of explanation, "I met Milena at the summer solstice festival. She actually kind of helped me make the decision to stay in town, and...in a way...Milena is kind of responsible for Ian and me."

Milena shook her head hard. "Oh no," she said. "I had nothing to do with it. I can't take any credit at all, Gwen. In fact, you're responsible for me. I mean..." She blushed hard and shook her head before she tried again. "What I mean is, you're responsible for helping me get my life back. You're an inspiration." Milena looked to Jade and me, her eyes only skimming over Cal, before she said, "Gwen's account changed my life. I watched everything she posted, and she absolutely was the inspiration for me to get healthy and leave a very bad relationship. In fact, if it hadn't been for that, I wouldn't have had the self-confidence to go after my real estate license. So really, it's you I have to thank for everything."

The two women hugged, and I was afraid they would start crying. I glanced over their shoulders at Jade, who looked just as bewildered as I was. But there was something else in her eyes, too. The look she gave me was intensely serious, as if she was trying to tell me something. I'd get to the bottom of that later.

"Real estate license?" Gwen looked from Milena up to me. "Don't tell me Milena's been helping you with what I think she has." Gwen almost squealed. "I mean... Are you thinking...?"

Cal slapped me on the back. "Did you buy a house?" He didn't wait for an answer. Cal shook his head and laughed. "Leave it to you to beat me to it. I was just thinking the same thing."

"You were not."

"How could I not? No offense, Gwen." He smiled apologetically across the table. "But the old house is getting a little crowded. And if I'm going to be staying...it was definitely on my mind to spread out a little bit. Maybe I'll just come bunk with you."

"We'll discuss it. But first, I'm going to get us a round of drinks to celebrate my new digs."

"We were just about to celebrate as well," Jade said. "Cal has been officially cast as Ian."

I shook my head. The whole idea of the show was still weird and took some getting used to. But it was extra weird to have my little brother playing the role of my older brother. *Oh well, whatever made them happy.* "Congratulations," I said. Then, looking at Jade, I added, "Would you mind giving me a hand with the drinks?"

She nodded. I waited until she slid out of her seat and joined me. I didn't say another word until I walked up to the bar and placed our order with Aaron, the new guy who'd been working at the Grizzly Paw.

"A bottle of champagne, please," I told Aaron.

"And just a glass of sparkling water for me."

I shot Jade a glance out of the corner of my eye, but didn't say anything. Maybe it was a work thing; after all, she was technically working and it was only early afternoon.

The second Aaron had gone to fetch the bottle, I turned to Jade. "I had a lot of fun yesterday. I hope you're not too tired today."

"I had a great day too." For the first time since I'd walked into the Grizzly Paw, I was treated to her beautiful smile. "And I'm a little tired today, but it was totally worth it."

It was worth it. It would be worth not sleeping ever again, if I could have that kind of fun with her every day. Not that I could say that. Instead, I said, "I'd love to do it again sometime. Or maybe even dinner? I haven't been up to the new restaurant at the Springs resort. Have you tried it?"

"That would be nice," she said. "It would be nice to have somebody, I mean…a friend to do things with."

Shit. She still thought of me as a friend. Of course, that had been totally my fault. And it would be totally up to me to fix it.

"Or maybe," I reached for her hand, taking her first two fingers lightly in mine before continuing, "maybe as more than a friend?"

Right then, Aaron returned with the bottle and a tray of glasses. I dropped Jade's hand and reached for my wallet. I handed over my credit card and Aaron excused himself to run it through.

"I hope that wasn't too forward," I said. Jade smiled, but it was tight and controlled. "Honestly, I'm just tired of pretending that I don't really enjoy spending time with you, and more than that... Jade, I just really—"

"Can we talk later? I'd really like to talk about this tonight."

I nodded. "Okay. Of course. Maybe over dinner?"

"No. Come to my place. I'm renting a little house just off Main Street. I'll write down the address for you."

I agreed, signed my credit card slip and carried the tray back to the table to celebrate with everyone. I probably should've been more concerned at whatever was hidden in Jade's eyes, but all I could think about was having the chance to see her again. This time, alone. Where I was gonna make sure I told her exactly how I was feeling. The time for secrets was long over.

Chapter Eleven

JADE

I WAS JUST GOING to be honest. That was the best approach.

The truth was, Mitch needed to know about the baby. I, in fact, knew he had a right to know. So that's what I was going to do. I was going to tell him the truth. And as much as it hurt my heart to do it, I was going to tell him that he didn't need to worry about a thing.

And it would hurt.

Because more than anything, what I really wanted to tell him was that not only was I pregnant with his child, I wanted to be with him. And it wasn't an ideal situation, but...

I couldn't do that.

He'd made it clear he only wanted to be friends. And the last thing I wanted was for him to be with me because of the baby. I didn't need his pity.

Or anything from him.

I could do it on my own and that's exactly what I was going to tell him.

It seemed simple enough.

Right. Simple.

I adjusted the throw pillows on the couch for what had to be at least the tenth time. I should have just thrown them in the closet when I'd first moved in. The rental had come fully furnished, which was exactly what I'd needed at the time.

Obviously, the landlord had decorated with summer guests in mind. It wasn't that the decor was offensive in any way and truth be told, I was starting to get used to the beach-themed furnishings.

When I first moved in, I hadn't cared much because the whole arrangement was meant to be temporary, but now... well, I'd have to figure out a long-term solution at some point. Maybe get some new accent pieces, a new rug, and—*what was I thinking?* Decorative accents should be the least of my concerns. I was going to have to start thinking about rounded corners, and cribs and childproofing. Not candles and picture frames.

I really needed to get my head in the game.

I forced myself to stop pacing. I stood in the middle of the little living room and took a breath. I closed my eyes and forced myself to exhale slowly using some yoga breathing technique I'd learned years ago in a class I'd taken when I thought yoga might actually be a good idea. It only took me a few classes to change my mind on that particular opinion.

Yoga was most definitely not for someone who couldn't sit still for five minutes at a time and "shut her brain off" for even thirty seconds. It made me crazy, trying to force myself to relax and inevitably, I was more wound up when I left the class than when I went.

But now, the yoga breathing technique was actually coming in kind of handy.

One. Two. Three.

Inhale through the nose. And... "Ommmmm."

I focused on holding my mouth open in just the right position, and really forcing the om out on my exhale.

To my surprise, it actually felt good.

I did it again.

This time louder.

And again. And again, until part of me wanted to get down on the floor and sit in the lotus position. I might have done it too, if the knock on the door hadn't startled me. Flustered, I smoothed my hair back, straightened my shoulders and went to let Mitch in.

Judging by the grin on his face, he'd seen my little breathing exercise through the side window. "Did I interrupt something?"

I shook my head and dropped my forehead into my hand. "I'm sorry you had to see that. Come in." I waved him inside.

"I'm not." He took a few steps in before he turned around and stopped short.

I almost bumped into him, and for a moment I thought he might kiss me.

I sidestepped him and walked toward the kitchen. "Can I get you a drink?"

"I'd love a beer," he said. "If you've got one."

I did. I'd bought it after our night on the boat in hopes that he might come by. There was no way I could have guessed that he'd be in my home under such circumstances.

"Of course. Make yourself at home. I'll be right back."

The moment I was in the kitchen, I braced myself on the counter and took deep breaths in an effort to slow my heart rate. I'd handled major diva clients who demanded everything but the moon from me in contract negotiations, and they'd never put me off my game. In fact, I'd handled those very same contract negotiations without even breaking a sweat. I'd stood in front of hundreds of people to give speeches, no problem. But this?

This was threatening to become one of the hardest things I'd ever done.

You got this, Jade. No big deal. Tell him you're pregnant and you don't expect anything. Done. Easy.

Right.

Except, despite how much I hoped that's how the conversation would go, somehow I didn't think it would be quite that easy.

There was no putting it off for much longer.

I grabbed the beer and the mug of tea I'd made for myself earlier and went back out to the living room. Mitch wasn't sitting. Instead, he stood by the window, looking out onto the street. It was still light out and a steady stream of people made their way back from the beach to their rental homes.

He must have heard me come into the room. "It's nice to see," he said without turning around. "All the families spending their summers together." I came to stand next to him and handed him the bottle. He thanked me with a tip of his head and eyed my tea questioningly but didn't comment. "I remember those days."

For a minute, I had the stupid idea that maybe Mitch actually wanted to recreate that memory with a family of his own. But as soon as the idea came into my head, I pushed it out. That wasn't going to happen. I wasn't his type. I needed to remember that. Besides, now there was a baby to think about.

Just remembering why I'd invited him over made my stomach roll with nausea again. I took a shaky sip of my peppermint tea.

"Mitch, I need to—"

"I'm really glad you—"

We spoke at the same time.

"Sorry," I said.

"No. Ladies first. What were you going to say?"

This was it. All I had to do was open my mouth and tell him the truth. Easy. I took a breath. Better to get it over with.

But when I opened my mouth to blurt it out, I said instead, "Why don't you come and sit?"

He smiled and followed me to the small couch. It wasn't a very big living room, and there was only one other chair, but it was pushed so far into the corner it would be awkward for me to sit there. Besides, I needed the stability of the couch around me because the way I was feeling, I needed all the support I could get. Even if it was only superficial.

Even though it wasn't ideal to be in such close proximity, I settled into the corner of the couch, tucking my legs in underneath me. His knees were angled close to me. He seemed so at ease, I almost hated to ruin it.

"What were you going to say?" I asked him in a last-ditch effort to procrastinate.

He reached for my hand. "I was just going to say that it's nice to be able to—"

"I'm pregnant!" The second the words were out, I clapped my hand to my mouth and squeezed my eyes shut.

"I'm sorry?"

"I'm pregnant." I whispered the words this time and opened my eyes to see him staring at me.

"But…why…how…I don't—"

"It's yours."

God.

I had never really been one for subtlety, but even for me, this was a bit brash.

"I mean…well…" I sighed. "The baby is yours," I repeated weakly. "It must have happened the night of the summer solstice festival."

He looked away and shook his head before running his hands through his hair.

"I didn't mean to tell you like this," I said quickly. "I wanted to tell you…Well, I don't really know how I wanted to tell you. But I knew I had to."

"Um, yes."

"I know," I said, needing to say everything I needed to before I lost my nerve. "You have a right to know. Of course. But I want you to know that this shouldn't change anything—"

"Fuck, Jade." He pushed up from the couch and stalked over to the window before he turned around. "This changes everything. How could it not?"

It wasn't going to change anything—at least not for him—because I was determined not to let it. I'd made my choice. It didn't have to change things for him.

"Because." I kept my voice level. "Because this is my decision. My problem. And I don't expect you to…well, I don't want anything from you. I was only telling you because I thought it was the right thing to do and frankly, things have a way of getting out in a small town, so I wanted to be the one to tell you."

He snorted and shook his head again. "Well, that was considerate of you." He turned and marched over to the wall. For a second, I thought he might punch it, but then he spun on his heel and stared at me, hard. "What do you mean you don't want anything from me?"

I stood, but stayed close to the kitchen. "It means just what you think it means. I don't expect anything from you."

He took a few steps toward me. "This is my baby?"

I nodded.

He took a few more steps until he stood next to the couch. "And you don't expect anything from me?"

I nodded again.

"I know you're moving on and you don't want to be with me. And it's not like we were ever really together, so I don't expect you to—"

"Dammit, Jade. Really?" I'd never heard him so angry, didn't even know he was capable of it. But really, there was so much I didn't know about him. It was just another reason that what we were doing was the right thing. "What the hell are you thinking?"

I held up my hands in an effort to—what? Calm him? I wasn't scared of *him*. Not at all. But his reaction... He was just so angry. Not that I knew what to expect from him. A calm thank you for letting me know. Or good luck with your decision. Or maybe even a how are you doing? But I hadn't expected anger. Not at all.

"Mitch, it's fine. Really."

"No, Jade. It's not fine. Nothing about this is fine," he growled and then kicked the foot of the couch hard enough to move it along the floor. He turned and stormed out of my house. The mirror hanging by the window shook when he slammed the door and left me standing in the middle of the room, somehow feeling even more alone than ever before.

MITCH

A BABY.

Seriously? A baby?

What the hell?

How could that have happened?

Hell. I *knew* how it could have happened. I knew all too well that the night of the summer solstice festival when I'd gotten her alone and had that first taste of her lips on mine, there was no way I could have not let it happen. Especially when she wrapped her lean legs around me and kissed my neck, pressing her body into mine, showing me exactly how badly she wanted it to happen too. And then when she'd whispered into my ear that she was on the Pill and we didn't need to worry, and—

"Dammit, Mitch." I kicked a rock on the beach. When it

didn't move far enough, I bent down, picked it up and hurled it into the lake.

I'd left my car parked in front of Jade's house because there was no way I should be behind the wheel of a vehicle. So I'd started walking along the lakefront in the general direction of the McCormick cabin and the house I'd just bought earlier today.

Had that really only been a few hours ago?

It seemed like a lifetime ago. But life-changing news had a way of doing that to the perspective of time.

It altered everything.

Jade was wrong. This news changed *everything*.

How could it not?

A baby.

I was going to be a father.

Ha. The thought made me laugh out loud. Me. A father.

But why not? It wasn't that long ago that I'd decided to make a change and start getting real with my relationships. Start dating the right kind of girl. I laughed again. That hadn't exactly turned out as planned.

But it didn't matter. Did it?

Maybe life wasn't supposed to turn out the way I planned it. Besides, wasn't getting serious about having a real relationship only the first step to marriage and a family? Wasn't that exactly what I was trying to achieve by making the decisions I'd been making all summer?

But this wasn't my decision.

She was pregnant. We weren't even together. And she was having a baby.

I'd gone over to her house thinking I'd finally be able to tell her how I felt and actually start a relationship with her and… this.

It was too much to think about and way too much to wrap my head around.

I threw another rock and then another, grunting with each toss. Letting my muscles feel the exertion of throwing heavier and heavier rocks into the water. It felt good because it gave me something else to focus on. I totally lost track of how long I'd been standing at the water's edge throwing rocks, but when my arm finally grew sore, I dropped the last rock and started to walk again. It took me just over twenty minutes to get home along the water's edge. I passed my new house. And in just a few minutes more, I ended up on the beach in front of my family home.

I dropped to the sand and put my head in my hands.

"Hey. Mitch? Is that you?"

I lifted my head to see a female figure walking down the stairs from the house. I lifted an arm in greeting and a moment later, Chelsea sat down next to me.

"What are you doing out here? I didn't see your car."

"I walked." I dropped my head to my knees again.

"From town?"

I nodded.

"That's a long walk." I could hear the unasked questions in her voice, but I didn't bother answering any of them.

"Yup," was all I said in response.

We sat in silence for a moment. Chelsea moved her feet through the sand, burying her toes before uncovering them. Finally, she spoke again. "Mitch? Are you okay?"

I could have lied. I could have told her I was fine, everything was fine and everything would be fine, but what was the point?

"No." I lifted my head and looked at my sister. Her face was lit by the full moon. "I'm going to be a—" A thought hit me hard. I hadn't even asked Jade how she felt. If she was scared or sick or how she was feeling or... God. *I was such a dick.* I shook my head again and tried again with the only information I actually knew. "Jade's pregnant."

. . .

FOR THE NEXT HOUR, I told Chelsea everything, including how I thought I'd needed to date a certain kind of girl, and how that little experiment had failed miserably when I'd realized I was in love with Jade. How Jade didn't want me. How I'd screwed it all up. And how now—just when I thought it couldn't get any more screwed up—Jade was pregnant.

When I was finally finished, my shoulders slumped over. I crossed my arms over my knees and dropped my head down between them. Chelsea was silent for a moment. No doubt processing everything she'd just heard.

Finally, she exhaled loudly and chuckled. "Wow, Mitch. You've only been here half the time I have and you've gotten yourself into a way bigger mess than I could have even imagined. And everyone was worried about *me* being on the wrong path."

She laughed, but I knew it wasn't at me. I looked up and ran my hand through my hair. "I know," I said. "It's a terrible mess and I have no idea what I'm going to do."

Chelsea's laughter cut off abruptly. "What do you mean you don't know what you're going to do?" she demanded.

My smile faltered as I realized she was genuinely giving me shit. "About Jade," I said weakly. "And the baby. I don't know what I'm—"

"You seriously don't know what you're going to do?" She stared at me. "After everything you just told me, you still don't know what you're going to do about it all?" When I shook my head, she laughed again. This time, I didn't join her. "I thought you were supposed to be one of the smart ones? Everyone used to tell me how smart Mitch was. You're a teacher at a prestige private school, for bloody sake." She scoffed and kicked the sand with her foot. "Maybe it's one of those book smart things because you certainly don't know anything when it comes to women."

I stared at her for a moment. And then another. "What are you talking about? I know plenty." And I did, too. I knew that Jade wasn't interested in me. I knew that she didn't want anything from me when it came to the baby and I knew that she'd looked absolutely destroyed when I'd yelled at her a few hours earlier.

"Dammit." I closed my eyes, remembering the look on her pretty face when I'd raised my voice. Hell, the look on her face when she'd told me the news. She'd been terrified to tell me, that was clear. And no wonder, too. I'd been a first-rate asshole. "I screwed everything up," I told Chelsea when I could finally manage to formulate the words. "I was a total jerk."

She nodded in agreement. "I'd say."

"Thanks."

"Hey," Chelsea objected. "I'm not doing you any good by telling you what you want to hear. But I'll certainly do my best to tell you what you need to hear. And what you need to hear is that you screwed up. You were an ass, but that doesn't mean you can't fix it."

Right. *Fix it.* It sounded so simple. All I needed to do was fix it. But…fix what?

As if she knew what I was going to ask, Chelsea continued, "First, you need to decide what it is you want out of this. Do you want a relationship? Do you love her? Do you want to be with her even if there wasn't a baby?"

The questions hit me hard. But the answer to each of them was a resounding yes.

"And then you need to understand that what Jade needs and wants might be different than what your ideas are. And if you truly care about her, that won't matter. You'll be there for her no matter what."

I nodded, but I still wasn't sure I understood. I would,

though. As soon as I spoke with Jade. I jumped to my feet and brushed the sand off my jeans.

"Whoa." Chelsea jumped up next to me and grabbed my arm. "Where do you think you're going?"

"To talk to Jade. I need to make her—"

"You need to wait until the morning." Chelsea tugged me toward the house. "It's late. Feelings are raw. Get some sleep, Mitch, and in the morning I'll drive you over there so you can say all the things you need to. But give yourself a night."

I nodded. It was a good idea. In fact, for someone so young, Chelsea had a lot of good ideas. "When did you get so smart?" I asked her as I let her lead me up to the house.

She patted my hand. "Big brother, I've always been this smart. You've missed out."

Impulsively, I hugged her. I had missed out on a lot with both of my half-sisters. But I'd changed a lot from that stupid, self-absorbed teenager. I was no longer going to let my pride get in the way of going after what I wanted.

Chapter Twelve

JADE

AFTER A NIGHT of tossing and turning, I was up before the sun. I'd managed to get a few hours of sleep, but not much more than that before I finally gave in, wrapped a robe around me and went out to the kitchen to make myself a cup of tea.

Lying in my bed reliving the awful night before wasn't doing me any good. And if I had to close my eyes and see Mitch's face when he realized what I was telling him, one more time, I just might cry. And that was the last thing I wanted. I'd worked hard to keep my emotions in check. It was too easy to let them get in the way of any of the decisions I needed to make. I had some absolutely huge life choices coming down, and I needed a clear head. There was no room for emotion of any kind. Not yet.

I fired up my laptop and scrolled through the emails I'd largely ignored for the last few days. It was completely unlike me to give my work such little regard. Already the baby was messing with my career and it wasn't even a thing yet.

Maybe my mom had been right about everything. Relationships and everything that came with them were nothing but a distraction keeping me from achieving everything I was capable of.

No.

I couldn't believe that. I needed to refocus and regroup.

My inbox was full and it took me a few minutes to go through each email to flag and file them for follow up. It felt good to get back to a system, something I could control when everything else was spinning wildly. I'd almost made it through the entire inbox when one message caught my eye. It was from Los Angeles about the actress who was interested in playing the lead role in Mr. Summer. I clicked it open and started to read.

Bridget Murphy was a big deal on an Australian lifeguarding show, but was looking to break into the North American market. She was going to be in California to screen test for the part and if that went well, which they felt it would, Peter wanted to send her to Cedar Springs for an extended audition. I just needed to call and confirm the details.

I glanced at the clock. It was almost six a.m. For anyone else, I'd wait a few hours to make the call. But I knew Peter would be up. He was an earlier riser than I was, so I might as well start working.

I grabbed my cell phone and punched in Peter's number. He answered on the first ring.

"Give me some good news, Jade." Peter's voice came across the line.

It took a few seconds for me to realize what he was talking about, but only a few before dread filled me. "I was calling about Bridget Murphy. I just read your email." I made the split decision to completely ignore the fact that I still didn't have the script from Gwen and not only that, I'd completely dropped the ball on making it a priority. "She sounds promising. And I'm sure she'll test well. We can have her read with Cal McCormick. He's ready to sign on to play Ian."

"Cal McCormick?"

"Remember? I sent you a text that he wanted to audition. He read yesterday and he's absolutely perfect. Gwen agrees." Again, I'd dropped the ball on talking to Peter about Cal's audition. I'd meant to call him the day before to arrange for paperwork. For a moment, I was afraid Peter might not agree with me, but he had trusted me to make a lot of the decisions for the show, and casting Cal would be a decision I was prepared to defend.

"Good," Peter said. "Be sure to send the details over ASAP so we can get legal to put together a contract. It could make things interesting with Bridget. Not that I keep up with Australian gossip, but Bridget and Cal were the IT couple until pretty recently."

"Oh. I had no idea." I did vaguely remember hearing something about Cal ending a relationship recently, but I'd been more than a little preoccupied. "I'll have to talk to—"

"No. Don't say anything. This could be great press for the show." Peter sounded downright giddy. "Think about it. Ex-lovers working together on a show like this. It could be exactly the kind of free publicity we need to attract sponsorships and a higher budget. Yes. This could be perfect."

"I don't know, Peter. It sounds pretty—"

"Do not say a word, Jade. Not to Cal, not to anyone. We'll hold Bridget's audition and then send her up to you. We'll make sure to have a photographer up there to catch it. It'll be brilliant."

I didn't like it. Not at all. It was sleazy and underhanded, but as long as Peter was focused on it for a little bit, the heat would be off me, Gwen, and the script. "Okay," I said after a minute. "I won't say a word." I'd figure out how to mitigate that disaster later. "Let me know how it goes and I'll make sure to get Cal McCormick's details down to legal."

I was about to end the call when Peter's voice cut through

again. "And Jade?" I took a deep breath in. "It sure would be nice if Bridget could read from the actual script. Get that to me. Today."

I nodded even though Peter couldn't see me. I swallowed hard. "No problem at all. I'll have you something by the end of the day. And I think you're really going to like it."

"I better."

I disconnected the call and ignoring the early hour, immediately dialed Gwen's cell phone. The time for a soft approach was over.

It took Gwen a few rings to pick up, but the second her sleepy voice came over the line, I said, "Get dressed. I'm picking you up in fifteen minutes. We have work to do and I'm not taking no for an answer."

"What? Jade? Is that you?"

I took a sip of tea before I repeated myself. "Fifteen minutes, Gwen. You're going to finish that script today, and I'm going to help. No cell phones, no Internet, no distractions—just the two of us and a laptop until it's finished."

"Where are we going?"

"I'll take care of it," I said. "Don't worry about anything. Just bring yourself, your laptop, and any notes you have."

As we were talking, I had already clicked through a few websites on my computer and was in the process of making an online reservation for a room at the Springs resort. We were going to disappear completely off the grid until the work was done. It was a technique I had used only once before with one of my particularly distracted author clients who was past deadline. Only that time, I didn't join the author, but made all the arrangements and drove her to the hotel. This time, I was going in, too. I needed to keep Gwen on task. And the fact that I'd be completely cut off from my life and my own dramas was only an added bonus.

"I don't know, Jade...I have a lot of things to—"

"I will not take no for an answer, Gwen. You're overdue. Let Ian know I'm going to pick you up in twenty minutes and under no circumstances will you be returning home until it's done." I hung up and started getting ready myself.

I'd promised Peter a script, and dammit, I was going to deliver. I powered off my phone and tucked it into the kitchen drawer. Besides, a day of distractions was exactly what I needed. I might be helping Gwen get her script finished, but I was going to use the time to figure out my future.

MITCH

I WAS positive I'd never be able to sleep. Not with so much on my mind. Not when every fiber of my being wanted to jump out of bed and run to her house to throw myself at the mercy of her forgiveness. I fully expected to toss and turn all night, counting down the hours until it was light enough to go to her.

Which was why I was shocked when my eyes finally opened at nine a.m. I jumped out of bed, showered and dressed as quickly as I could and was about to sneak out of the house when Chelsea stopped me.

"I'm glad to see you at least listened to me about waiting until morning." She handed me a cup of coffee, but I put it down on the table.

"No time for coffee, Chels. I can't wait another minute. I slept in and I need to see her. I need to make it right."

"Make what right?" Cal appeared, groggy from sleep. "What did I miss?"

"Everything." Chelsea rolled her eyes and jumped up to sit on the kitchen counter. "Seriously, how do you sleep so late?"

"It's called jet lag, smart ass. It's like tomorrow afternoon in my world."

I started to do the mental math in my head, but gave up with a shake. "Whatever," I said. "You two have fun sorting that out. I have things to do."

"Right," Cal said. "You have to make something right. Sounds like a woman problem. Seems to be going around. What did *you* screw up?"

Something in my little brother's voice caught my attention. Was there more to Cal leaving Australia than he'd said? I wanted to ask, but…I glanced at the door and caught Chelsea's eye. She'd clearly noticed the change in tone in Cal as well. She gave me a look that said *you can wait a few more minutes to make sure your brother is okay*. With a sigh, I grabbed my cup of coffee and sat at the table.

"What's going on, little brother? You sound like you have a story to tell."

Cal sat across from me and laughed in his casual it's nothing I can't handle kind of way, but I knew better. And judging by the look on Chelsea's face, so did she. Cal was the free spirit, easygoing brother, but that didn't mean he didn't hurt. In many ways, he fell harder and hurt deeper than my other brothers and me.

"I thought you said you broke up with Bridget." Chelsea joined us at the table.

Cal's laugher died and he dropped his head in his hands. "I did. But only because I didn't have a choice. She wasn't the woman I thought she was. She wasn't the woman I was in love with."

I took a sip of my coffee and waited until Cal continued.

"I honestly thought that what Bridget and I had was special. I thought she was the one." He looked at Chelsea when he said that. "I was going to marry her. It was going to be forever. It really was."

"What happened?" she asked.

"Were you an asshole?" I couldn't help but ask it even

though I knew that was my reason for heartbreak, not Cal's. My little brother shot me a look.

"She betrayed me," he said simply.

"Another man?" Because of what our father had put us all through by having an entire secret family, all of the McCormick children had a very low tolerance for cheating. And if she'd been unfaithful, I didn't blame him for a second. "What a—"

"No." Cal cut me off. "I wanted to get into acting," he started to explain. "I was getting tired of just standing in front of the camera. I wanted to do more. When I told her about my plans, she seemed really supportive and even offered to talk to her director about getting me on the show. She's the star of Beach Bodies. It's like the Australian version of Baywatch," he explained to me.

"I'm familiar."

If Cal noticed my impatience, he didn't say anything, but continued on with the story. "I was really excited," he said. "In fact, when I was getting set to go on a few auditions, she told me not to because something was going to happen with her show. I passed up a lot of opportunities that my agent lined up for me. And finally my agent dropped me because of it. So when that happened, I pressed the issue with her."

"Don't tell me," Chelsea said. "Was she just trying to spare your feelings?"

"What?" Cal shook his head. "No. Not at all. I ran into the producer at a club one night and asked him straight out if he thought I might have a chance to get on the show soon. You know what he said to me?"

Chelsea and I both shook our heads.

"He laughed. He looked right in my face and laughed at me. Then he proceeded to tell me that Bridget had come to him and told him I was probably going to ask about getting on the show, and when I did, he should lie and say something nice because under no circumstances should he hire me to be on the show because of how terrible I was."

I almost spat out my coffee. "She said what? But you're not terrible. I mean, Jade just said how awesome you were." Just speaking her name out loud hurt my heart and reminded me that I should go as soon as possible. But I did my best to be a good brother and listen.

"In fact, not only did she tell him how terrible I was, she said that she'd quit the show altogether if he hired me."

"Why would she do that?"

"Jealous," Chelsea answered with a nod of her head. "Sounds like jealousy to me. She probably saw your star rising and didn't want you to succeed without her."

"Or more than her," I added. "That's shitty, little brother. Sorry."

Cal nodded and ran a hand through his shaggy hair. "Well, it is what it is, right? Better I found out this way though, right? I mean, before I asked her to marry me."

"You were going to do that?" Cal nodded and Chelsea got out of her seat to give him a hug. "I'm really glad you didn't. You need a nice girl."

A nice girl.

Like Jade.

I swallowed down the rest of my coffee and put my mug down harder than I intended before I stood. "You're exactly right, Cal. It's good you found out about her true colors now. And Chelsea's right too," I continued. "You need a good girl. Just like I do. And you'll find one, too. Just like I did."

Chelsea beamed and clapped her hands together.

"Which is why I need one of you to give me a lift into town. Now, if possible. I can't wait any longer. I can't let her get away."

Chapter Thirteen

JADE

IT WAS my first time up at the Springs resort. I'd heard plenty about how relaxing and serene it was, and I was not disappointed. I'd rented a room and left specific instructions not to let anyone know we were there. Not that anyone would know we were there, but I could imagine Ian trying to find Gwen, and I didn't want Gwen going anywhere until we were done with the script.

To get to our room, we walked down a long hallway that was completely glass on one side, exposing the mountain right outside. It was the coolest effect because it felt as if we were actually on the mountain. Which in a way, we were. The pools were located on the other side of the hotel. I didn't tell Gwen, but I'd packed us some bathing suits that we were only going to use as a treat when we were finished with our work. Hopefully, by then we'd deserve a little relaxation.

"This room is amazing. Can we order room service? I'm starving."

I walked in after her and opened the curtains to let in the

sunshine and the beautiful mountain view. I turned and pointed to Gwen's laptop. "Open it up. Let's see what you've got first, and then we'll order."

"Oh, come on," Gwen whined. "We really should get some food first, don't you think? I write so much better after I've eaten."

"That's crap, and you know it. You write better after you exercise, and I'll be happy to go down to the gym with you and type while you dictate to me from the treadmill if that's what it takes, but we absolutely need to get this done, Gwen. I don't understand what's going on."

Gwen sighed and smoothed her hair back. "Okay." She flopped down on the bed and pulled her laptop over, firing it up. She clicked a few buttons and pushed it over to me. "Here you go. This is what I have."

I half expected to see a blank page, the way Gwen had been carrying on, but I was surprised when I saw a full document. I settled into the armchair by the window and read through everything.

When I was done, I looked up at Gwen, who lay on her back, staring at the ceiling. "I don't understand," I said. "This is good." I glanced down at the laptop again to see whether maybe I was reading some other script because there was, in fact, nothing wrong with the one I was reading. I'd said it, and I meant it. What Gwen had written was good.

"I don't think so." Gwen rolled over on her stomach and looked at me. "It's too...I don't know..."

"I don't think it's too anything. It's great. Especially for a first episode—the teaser right at the end that you'd actually known Ian all along, it's absolutely—"

"Harsh." Gwen dropped her head into the pillow.

"I was going to say perfect." I closed the laptop, left it on the chair, and joined my friend on the bed. "It's your story," I said gently, realizing what the problem likely was.

"That's the whole problem." Gwen groaned. She looked up again. "I mean, I know my story. I know our story. After all, I lived it. Hell, I even wrote about it. I know it. But somehow writing about it like this, so I can watch it all play out again on the screen, it just seems too…I don't know…"

"Harsh," I finished for her, using her own word.

"Yes." She nodded. "It's really harsh." She pulled herself up to sitting and crossed her legs in front of her. "Was it really all that bad? I mean, was I really such a bitch to do that to Ian? To play him that way? And all for stupid social media?" She covered her face with her hands and shook her head. "I'm horrible."

"You're not horrible." I had to take more than a little of the responsibility for the deception Gwen had played on Ian. As her agent, I'd pushed her to follow through on it, to take it further and ultimately, it became a secret too twisted for Gwen to unwind easily. Fortunately, the love between Gwen and Ian was real, and it was strong. It was their love that saved them, brought them back together and was the entire reason why their show was going to be so damn good. A love like that was incredibly rare to find.

I felt a pang of jealousy, but I didn't have time to entertain it. Gwen was the priority.

"How can he possibly love me after all that I did?" Tears slipped down my friend's face. "I think I could kind of ignore it before, push it behind me and not think about the terrible things I did. But now…I just don't understand how I could have done all that. And I really don't understand how Ian could possibly want to be with me after all of it."

I gave Gwen a moment to cry, but only a moment before I rubbed her shoulder and then squeezed gently. "I know you think it's harsh," I said. "But try to remember that what you wrote is only the start of the story. It's literally episode one. You still have so much to write and as you do, you'll be able to revisit all of the wonderful things, too."

I knew what Gwen was going to say, what the new objection would be. So I headed it off.

"You're going to go through this again," I said. "When you get closer to the end, there will be all kinds of feelings." Gwen nodded. We both knew what I was talking about. If Gwen was going to write the script truthfully, she'd have to revisit painful memories of when Ian discovered the truth. That had been a hard night, and no doubt it would be even harder to recreate for the screen. "But then you'll get through the other side to the wonderful coming together of your love," I said. "Remember that you and Ian are the lucky ones. Your love is strong and it not only made it through the adversity, it's thriving. Focus on the good parts of your story. Don't dwell on what you can't change."

It was good advice. For a few minutes, neither of us said anything. We just let my words and the moment settle in. Finally, Gwen's tears dried up and she sat straighter. She refastened her ponytail and wiped her face. "You're right," she said. "I'm just being silly."

"I don't think it's silly to feel passionately and care about what you're working on. I don't think that's silly at all." I gave her a hug. "But it is silly to question your love. What you and Ian have together is special. We should all be so lucky."

"You're right."

"You know I am." I laughed. "Now, since the first episode is done, let's get to work on a few more. I don't want to have to kidnap you again."

MITCH

"JADE!" I knocked on her door again. Still no answer.

Where the hell could she be?

The idea that she was inside her house and simply ignoring me was simply not an option.

But it could be.

"Jade!" I knocked louder before I glanced around. A few families walked down the sidewalk, arms loaded with inflatables, picnic baskets, and chairs. I gave them a little wave and tried to look as if I belonged there. The moment they'd moved a safe distance down the sidewalk, I turned and hammered on the door again. "Open up. We need to talk! Please, Jade!"

When there was still no movement inside, I turned and sat down hard on the front steps. I'd already dialed her number a dozen times. No answer.

I punched in the numbers again.

Her voicemail message came on almost immediately.

"Dammit, Jade. Where are you?"

I admitted defeat, at least for the time being, and went in search of a coffee. She either really wasn't home, or really didn't want to talk to me. Either way, I'd be back to try again because one thing was for sure: I was not giving up.

I left my car where it was in front of her house and walked the short distance to Main Street and Dream Puffs bakery. I ordered a black coffee and a muffin that smelled too delicious for my empty stomach to pass up and found the only open table, sandwiched between an elderly couple, heads bent together as they worked on a crossword puzzle, and a couple about my age.

Couples were everywhere. I tried not to feel the pinch of bitterness that instead of sitting there alone, I should be there with Jade, as a couple of our own.

As I sipped my coffee, I made a mental list of all the places she could possibly be. It was a small town; it's not as though there were a lot of places to be. Unless, of course, she was avoiding me. Or worse, she'd left. The thought filled me with panic. No. Surely she wouldn't have left town. Not with the show getting ready to shoot. It meant too much to her.

Gwen would know.

I didn't know why I hadn't thought of it earlier. I pulled out my phone and was just about to find Gwen's number when movement at the table next to me caught my attention.

"I got her, babe," the man said to his girlfriend. He reached down and picked up a baby carrier that I hadn't noticed earlier. Inside was the tiniest human I'd ever seen.

I didn't mean to eavesdrop or intrude on the couple, but I couldn't help but watch as the man slowly and gently unfastened the baby's buckles and lifted her from the seat.

She was impossibly small, especially in the man's arms. The woman reached over and stroked the baby's cheek before she looked up at the man. "I still can't believe she's ours," she said to him. "She's just so beautiful."

"Just like her mama." The man bent and kissed the woman on the lips.

It was an intimate moment and I never should have been watching it, but I couldn't seem to move my eyes from the scene before me that could so easily be me and Jade and our own baby in a few months.

The thought should have scared me. Hell, it would have scared me at any other time. But at that moment, not knowing whether I'd lost Jade forever or whether I could still win her back, there wasn't anything I wanted more than to play out a similar scene with her and our child.

"She's pretty incredible, isn't she?" It took me a moment to realize the man holding the baby was speaking to me. He was alone with the child; the woman must have excused herself to the bathroom while I was lost in my private thoughts.

"Sorry," I mumbled. "I didn't mean to—"

"No." The man shook his head. "It's all good. Babies have

a way of doing that to people. My name's Seth." He shifted the child and offered his hand to me. "You're one of the McCormick brothers, aren't you? I've seen you around town. I actually helped your brother put the new boats in. But I'm sorry to say I've been a little too preoccupied with my new family to make a better effort to welcome you all. It's good to meet you."

"I'm Mitch."

"My girlfriend Cynthia owns the General Store, and this here is Lindy. She's named after Cynthia's mother, Linda, who just passed away."

"I'm sorry to hear about your loss." I focused on the baby. "She's...well, she's just...so small."

Seth laughed. "She is. She was born almost two months too early. But we're lucky. She only had to spend a few days in the hospital. She's strong. Like her mama."

She was so incredibly small. I couldn't stop staring at her. "That's great," I said. It felt inadequate, but it was the only thing I could say, and then I realized something Seth had said a moment earlier. "Did you say Cynthia was your girlfriend? So, you're not married?" I wasn't sure why it mattered, but for whatever reason, it did.

Seth laughed and then cuddled the baby a little closer, making a soothing sound. "No," he said. "We're not married. There wasn't time. I mean, by the time I found out about her." He gestured with his chin down at the sleeping bundle. "It was a couple months in already, and then I had to convince Cyn that I loved her and then...well...unfortunately, Cynthia's mom was very sick. Sadly, she passed away."

"Oh. I'm so sorry."

"Thanks." Seth nodded once. "It was a hard time, for sure," he said. "It still is hard, actually. And with the stress of everything, Cynthia went into labor early. Which, I guess, turned out to be a good thing since Lindy here is just so perfect and thankfully was healthy enough to come home. It could have been so different, right?"

I nodded, but I had no idea what Seth was talking about. "What do you mean she was a few months along by the time you found out? You had to convince her that you loved her?" That story sounded a little too familiar.

"Let's just say that this little miracle wasn't entirely planned." The woman, Cynthia, returned to the table and stuck out her hand. "Hi," she said. "I'm Cynthia. I see Seth here is giving away all our secrets."

They laughed. "I'm Mitch."

"I know." She shrugged. "Small town, sorry."

"No problem." I scooted my chair over to join them at their table. "And I'm sorry if I'm asking personal questions. I just…" I wondered how much I should say. "Well, it's crazy. My friend actually just found out he was going to be a father, but he's not technically with the baby's mother. It's kind of complicated."

"It always is." Seth laughed.

"Do you—I mean, does your *friend* love the woman?"

I eyed her, but continued to play along. I didn't know how much Jade had told, or whether she was going to tell anyone at all. Hell, I didn't know anything.

After a moment, I nodded. "He does."

Seth laughed again, this time startling the baby, who started to stir. Cynthia reached out, and Seth handed her the child before continuing. "Sorry to laugh," he said. "It's just that if your friend loves her, it just seems kind of simple." He glanced at his girlfriend. "I mean, it's never completely simple. But it is easier if there's love. Way easier."

"That's very true." Cynthia nodded. "I'd tell your *friend* to make sure the woman knows how much he loves her and that he'll do whatever he needs to in order to support her and love her through everything. Babies are a blessing, to be sure. But, if they're unplanned, they tend to come with some unexpected challenges as well."

Right. I could totally see that. I nodded despite the fact that I still had so many questions.

"It's not easy, man." I looked at Seth, who looked very serious. "But it's totally worth it. Tell your...friend," he winked at Cynthia, "to give it everything he has. Otherwise he'll regret losing something he may not have even been sure he wanted at the time. Looking back, I could never have forgiven myself if I hadn't tried everything I could to make sure Cynthia knew how much I loved her and our unborn baby. Life changing, for sure. But worth all of it."

We chatted for a few more minutes, the conversation shifting to the more neutral topic of Gwen and Ian's show, and of course the marina and how things were doing generally in town. Although I was in the conversation, I couldn't help but let my mind drift back to what Seth had said. And I knew what I had to do.

I was in love with her. Of that I had no doubt.

Now, I needed to do everything in my power to make sure Jade knew it, too.

Chapter Fourteen

JADE

IT TURNED out that it had only taken Gwen and me a few hours to finish up the scripts for the first five episodes and sketch out another four. And they were good. Really good. I was confident Peter would love them and we'd be able to start filming just as soon as the rest of the casting was decided upon. Despite our work being finished up, or maybe because of it, we decided to stay at the Springs for the rest of the day and enjoy all the amenities. After all, we deserved it after all the work we'd done.

The fact that I was trying to avoid my reality had nothing to do with it. At least that's what I kept telling myself. And I had no plans to tell myself any different, either. At least not until I'd finished soaking in the hot pool filled with naturally therapeutic waters and eating the delicious snacks that Jax, the amazing head chef, had prepared for us. Maybe then I'd be ready to deal with my reality.

But not even one minute before.

I tilted my head back against the stone and closed my eyes.

"This is amazing. Truly. I think we should make this a weekly ritual."

Across from me, Gwen groaned in agreement. "And the massages here are to die for, too."

"Seriously? Okay, definitely a weekly ritual then," I confirmed but then changed my mind. "Well, maybe only a monthly one. I'm not sure my checking account would like it."

"Monthly?" There was the sound of water splashing as Gwen sat up. I opened my eyes to see her staring at me. "Are you going to be around for a while then?" She didn't beat around the bush. "Is there maybe a certain someone keeping you here?" She wiggled her eyebrows and despite myself, I laughed.

"Honestly," I said. "I haven't decided yet. But I think I would like to." I waved my hands in the water, watching the bubbles dance around my skin. "I mean, I'll be here for the show."

"You know that's not what I meant." Gwen tilted her head and examined me. "Seriously, are you thinking of staying? Cedar Springs is a great place to live." She laughed. "Not that I really know, being new myself. But maybe we can discover it together. That would be fun, being the new girls together."

"You're hardly new," I said.

Gwen had been spending her summers in Cedar Springs since she was a kid. It was only after a long absence that she'd come back recently and fallen in love with Ian. So technically, she was only new to Cedar Springs as an adult, and considering she was so different from when she was a kid, she might as well be.

"We're getting off topic." Gwen sat up and moved through the water so she sat across from me. "Are you going to stay or what? And I don't just mean for the show. Like, permanently? Are you staying?"

I tried to laugh but it came off weak and unsure. "What's with all the questions? I feel like I'm on trial."

"Hardly. But I would like answers."

I wanted to answer her. Gwen was the closest thing I ever had to a real girlfriend, someone I could confide in and ask for guidance. And if I could ever use some guidance, now would be the time. I closed my eyes and swallowed hard. It probably wouldn't hurt to talk it all out with Gwen. In fact, it might really help. Besides, Mitch knew the truth now. Not that it mattered because it was so clear that he wanted nothing to do with talking about it. I really had nothing else to lose. "It's complicated," I said. "And it's kind of a long story."

"I've got nothing but time. Spill," Gwen commanded.

I didn't need to be asked twice. If Gwen was willing to listen, I was ready to talk. "I'm pregnant."

Gwen didn't say anything right away. She blinked. Once and then again. "Pardon me? I must have water in my ears because I could have sworn you just said you were pregnant and I know that just the other day you told me in no uncertain terms that—"

"I am." I swallowed hard. "I'm sorry I lied to you. But I just wasn't ready to tell."

"Wow. So…it's for sure?"

I nodded. "Deanna confirmed it. It's still really new, like maybe only five weeks. But it's happening. I'm going to have a baby."

"So you are having it?"

It was a blunt question, but I could appreciate it. I nodded. All of the uncertainty of the last few days vanished. Of course I was keeping the baby. No matter what my mom thought, no matter what it might do to my career, no matter what Mitch decided to do. I was definitely going to be a mother and that thought made my heart happy. "Absolutely."

With a big splash, Gwen threw her arms around me and

squeezed. "I'm so excited for you. You will be a fantastic mother, and you totally have to stay in Cedar Springs now. I mean, Mitch—it is Mitch's?"

I splashed in my friend's direction. "Of course."

"What did he say? Is he excited?"

The happiness I'd felt a moment earlier evaporated, and my heart sank. "Not entirely," I said. "He kind of...well, he got kind of mad."

Gwen used her hands to push up out of the water and sit on the edge of the hot pool. "Mad? That doesn't sound like Mitch. Why would he be mad? I mean...I assume none of this was planned, and...are you guys even together?"

The confusion that lined my friend's face mirrored what I felt inside. The whole situation was a mess. Were we together? No. He wasn't interested in me. Not like that. Well, not for a relationship anyway. He'd liked me plenty for some fooling around, but when it came to being worthy of a relationship... I didn't want to think about it. It hurt too much.

"No," I answered. "We're not. He was dating Evie."

"Evie?"

"They're not together or anything, but they went out right after he told me I wasn't his type."

"That's bullshit." Gwen kicked her feet in frustration. "I've seen you guys together. You're perfect for each other. And he knows it, too. He's just being stupid. Men are so stupid sometimes."

I couldn't disagree with that statement, but men weren't the only ones who could make bad decisions. I shrugged. "I also might have told him that he didn't have to worry about it because I didn't want anything from him."

"You did what?"

I looked down at the water swirling around me. "I told him that whatever I decided, I'd take care of everything, and he didn't have to worry about it."

"And that's why he got mad." It wasn't a question, but I nodded anyway. "Shit, Jade."

I pulled myself out of the water and sat next to my friend. "I know. I kind of made a mess of that, didn't I?"

"I'd say so."

We sat in silence for a few minutes. I moved my feet through the warm water, letting the bubbles flow over my legs. The therapeutic waters felt good—I could happily sit in them all day—but as relaxing as they were, they weren't going to be the solution to my problems. No matter how badly I wished they would.

"So how did you leave things?" Gwen finally asked.

"He slammed out of my house, and I haven't seen him or heard from him since." It hurt me to say the words. "I told you, he was mad."

"Of course he was mad, Jade. You told him you didn't want anything from him." Gwen spun around so she faced me. "Did you even ask him what he thought about it all? Or did you just treat the baby like a problem he didn't need to concern himself with?"

I didn't need to answer.

"Jade." Gwen grabbed my hand. "I don't know Mitch all that well myself, but I know him well enough to know that he would have been hurt by that because he's not the type of guy to *not worry about it*." She made air quotes with her fingers. "And for you to assume he would just walk away from you and the baby, that's hurtful."

Gwen's words hit home. I *had* been cold. But I hadn't meant to be, not at all. "I was just trying to protect myself," I said. Tears pricked at my eyes and my throat started to swell with emotion. "I just didn't want him to think I did it on purpose and I know the baby will mean my career will…well, I don't want it to ruin everything for Mitch, too."

"Ruin everything?" Gwen grabbed me by the upper arms

and shook me gently. "Is that what you think, Jade? That the baby will ruin things?"

Unshed tears burned my eyes.

I will not cry. I *cannot* cry.

A tear escaped and ran down my cheek.

Dammit.

I swiped at my face, hoping Gwen wouldn't see.

She did.

"Hey," Gwen said gently. "Talk to me, Jade. What's going on? I mean, I get it…you must be completely overwhelmed with this news, but a baby isn't going to ruin anything. Why would you think that?"

"Because it's true." The tears came fast now and I didn't bother trying to stop them. "My career, my…well, everything."

"That's ridiculous." Gwen wiped my cheek. "It's not the fifties. Women today have careers and children—you must know that."

I shrugged. Logically, I did know that, but it was one thing to know what a baby would do to your life and another thing to know it. I'd never advance the way I wanted to because there would always be sick days and school plays and appointments and something that was more important than a client. I'd be passed over for promotions and raises, and that would be okay because my child would be more important. *But what if one day…*

"It's not just my career." I wiped my eyes and tried to force a smile. "It's just that…I don't want to do it on my own, Gwen. I don't want to be a single mom. I don't want to do all the midnight feedings by myself and celebrate first steps on my own and go to recitals and—"

"Whoa." Gwen's smile was kind and despite the fact that I knew I was being crazy, now that I'd started, I couldn't seem to stop myself. "You're getting ahead of yourself. No one is saying that you can't have it all. A baby, a career, a relationship—you can have it all, Jade. You know that, right?"

More than anything, I wanted to say yes. But I couldn't help but hear my mother's voice in my ear telling me I was ruining my life, the same way having me had ruined hers. Men, children…love. It would be the end of everything.

"Jade?" Gwen prompted when I didn't answer right away. "Tell me that you understand that a child will only make your life better, not worse. You do know that, right?"

"I do." I nodded. "I really do. It's just that…my mother always told me to stay away from all of it." I laughed a little, realizing how crazy it sounded. "She taught me to chase my dreams and not to let a man or a child come between me and what I wanted."

Gwen listened for a minute and squeezed my hand. "And what if that is exactly what you want?"

I thought about that for a moment. What if that was everything I wanted? Having a family had never been part of my dreams before, but maybe that was just because I didn't even realize it should be. What if this was fate's way of telling me that love and family was more important than a job title or a raise or—

A fresh round of tears started, only these were different.

"Jade?"

I nodded. "I think you're right, Gwen." I smiled through the hot tears that streamed down my cheeks. "I think this might be exactly what I want."

Gwen laughed. "Then why are you crying?"

I joined her in laughter. "I don't know. I've never cried so much in my whole life."

"Hormones," Gwen said matter-of-factly, sparking a fresh round of giggles from me.

I let myself laugh because it felt good and more than that, it felt good to release myself from the confinement of years of thinking I shouldn't allow myself to want a family of my own, when deep down it was what I'd always craved.

It was freeing, but a new realization came quickly after that.

Not only did I want the baby—I wanted the family. I wanted Mitch.

And I'd screwed up everything.

MITCH

TALKING to Seth and Cynthia had made me feel better. It had also made me even more anxious. After they'd excused themselves to put their baby down for a nap, I had stayed in the bakery as long as I could before finally I needed to get up and get some fresh air.

Not hearing from Jade was making me crazy. I'd tried calling her a dozen more times, choosing not to leave a voicemail after the first few. I'd sent her text messages, but if she'd read them, she wasn't replying.

Why was she ignoring me? Was she that upset?

"Dammit, Jade." I muttered under my breath and kicked at a stone on the rocky lakeshore. Walking along the beach had always made me feel better when I was a teenager. It had given me the peace to think about whatever it was that was bothering me. Of course, when I was younger, my biggest problem had been which girl to take to the various festivals and dances in town. Now, all these years later, walking along the shoreline wasn't helping me find the answers I needed. The only thing that could do that was Jade herself.

I pulled my phone out again, prepared to call her one more time, but a text message flashed across the screen:

Where are you? Get to the Dockside ASAP.

Ian. It was the third message he'd sent. No doubt he was pissed because I hadn't shown up to help out. Which, I had to admit, was pretty shitty of me. After all, Ian was counting on me. But how could I be expected to concentrate on work of any kind when Jade was missing? Then again, maybe it would be a good distraction. And maybe Ian could ask Gwen if she knew anything. Yes. Why hadn't I thought of that before?

I turned around and jogged in the opposite direction, toward the Dockside.

"It's about time you got here," Ian hollered to me from the office the moment I stepped onto the dock.

I shrugged.

"Have you seriously been ignoring my texts all day?" Ian asked when I got closer. "What the hell?"

"I'm sorry," I said. "What's the big emergency?" All the boats were out from the dock, and I could see the two jet skis ripping around in the lake. If everything was rented, he couldn't need the help too badly. "Looks like you have things under control around here."

"I wanted to show you something." Ian put his arm around my shoulder and moved to lead me inside the office. "Or should I say…someone."

"Jade?" I all but pushed Ian out of the way to get inside. "I've been looking everywhere for—" The words died on my lips when I saw who waited for me inside. "Dec?" A smile stretched across my face when I realized my little brother stood across from me. "Dammit, Declan. What are you doing here?" I pulled my brother into a strong hug. It had been way too long since I'd seen him.

"Hey. Good to see you, man." Declan slapped my back and hugged me in return. "It's been way too long."

"No shit." I took a step back and shook my head in wonderment. "Seriously. What the hell are you doing here? I thought you were in Botswana or something saving the world."

"Haiti," Dec corrected me. "And I don't know about the world, but I'm sure doing my best for as many as I can."

My little brother was truly the nicest, most considerate person with the biggest heart. Never in my life had I met anyone who'd come close to sharing the type of compassion Declan demonstrated on a regular basis.

"What are you doing here?" I asked again.

Dec pretended to look offended before he chuckled. "I kept hearing about how much fun you all were having, and there was no way I was going to let you have all that fun without me. Besides, I needed to properly meet my new sister-in-law-to-be." He elbowed Ian in the ribs. "I can't believe you finally convinced someone to marry you, old man."

"Ha. I'm hardly old, little brother. And as for Gwen, I was just waiting for the right one. And man, is she ever the right one."

Seeing the love shine in my big brother's eyes sharpened the sting of the pain in my gut.

"Hey," I interrupted. "Speaking of your lovely bride-to-be...does she know where Jade might be?"

"Jade?" Declan wiggled his eyebrows, but I ignored him.

"Of course she knows," Ian said. "Jade picked her up this morning, and they went up to the Springs."

"The Springs? Like the new resort?"

"The one and only," Ian confirmed. "Something about Gwen needing to finish the scripts, and Jade wasn't going to let her leave or have any distractions until they were done. No phones, no nothing. They left bright and early, and honestly, I don't expect them home until late. Gwen's been struggling a little bit with this, and I don't know why. But I'm sure Jade will help her figure it out."

"I'm sure she will." I nodded, but I was already putting a plan in motion to drive up there and find her. It made sense that she hadn't answered my calls or text messages if she didn't have a phone. Assuming she didn't have hers either, if Gwen hadn't been allowed to take one. Maybe if I got up there, I could convince someone to tell me what room she was in and surprise her with—

"Don't even think about it." Ian interrupted my train of thought. "They need to get the script done, Mitch. Do not go interrupt them."

I glared at my brother. "Why would you think I'd do that?"

"I see that look on your face." Ian shook his head and crossed his arms. "There's no way I'm letting you go up there."

There was no point trying to fool him. Ian clearly had me figured out. A direct approach was what was warranted. "Look, Ian. I need to talk to her. Like, I really need to talk to her. I don't think you understand."

"I do."

"Who is Jade?"

"Screw this." I wasn't going to stick around and have this conversation. I tried to push past my big brother, but Ian shoved me back. I stumbled backward and crashed into a rack of life jackets. "Get out of my way, Ian."

"No." Ian shook his head and stood his ground.

I'd gone up against my brother before, but not since we were teenagers. I had lost as many of those fights as I'd won. We were pretty evenly matched, but that was before I had something to lose. This time, I had everything to lose, and I was not going to let it happen.

"I don't know what's going on with you and Jade, but this is not happening. Not like this."

"Ian, I'm warning—"

"Who is Jade?" Tired of being ignored, Declan grabbed my shoulder and pulled me back, putting himself between his two older brothers. "Seriously, who is Jade and what is going on here?" Declan looked between the two of us, waiting for answers.

"Jade is…she's…" I drifted off, unsure of how to describe exactly who Jade was and more importantly, what she was to me.

"Jade is the woman Mitch is in love with."

"What?"

"What?"

We both spoke at the same time, turning to Ian.

"I'm what?"

"Wait," Dec said. "You're in love?" He slapped my back. "Congratulations, man. That's awesome. Now I have two future sisters-in-law to meet."

"What?" I spun around to my younger brother. "No. You don't. I mean…"

It wasn't a bad idea. In fact, it was a damn good idea. But I couldn't get ahead of myself. First things first. I focused on Ian again. "What are you talking about—I'm in love with Jade? What do you know about it?"

"I'm not blind, brother." Ian laughed and I was so wound up, I would have taken a swing at him just to wipe the grin off his face if I hadn't wanted to hear what he had to say. "It doesn't take a genius to see how you look at her. You've been in love with her from the very first day you met her at the summer festival. Hell, I was a little preoccupied with my own drama, but I still noticed."

The festival. Just the mention of it brought back a rush of amazing memories from that night. She'd looked so sexy, and when she opened her mouth to challenge me, I'd wanted her on the spot. Maybe Ian was right. Maybe I had fallen in love with her that night. At any rate, we'd always have a souvenir of that particular festival and the night we met.

I shook my head. "She's pregnant." I blurted it out, needing to tell someone.

"She's what?" Ian's eyes grew wide.

"Damn. I'm going to be an uncle?" Dec slapped his thigh. "Now I'm really glad I came back."

"Who's going to be an uncle?" Cal walked into the office. The three of us turned to stare at him.

"Seriously?" Declan shook his head at Cal. "Sometimes I think it's a good thing you make a living with your looks because you're not the brightest of the bunch."

"Good to see you, too, brother." Cal punched him playfully on the shoulder. "Seriously, who's going to be an—ahh, I see." Cal laughed and rephrased the question. "Okay…so who is going to be a daddy?"

"Better, smart guy," Declan said with a shake of the head.

"So?" Cal ignored him in favor of getting the information he wanted.

Ian hitched a thumb in my direction and Cal's eyes got wide. "You haven't changed a bit, have you? Are you even dating—"

I shut him up with a punch to the mouth that sent my brother reeling backward.

"Whoa." Ian grabbed me through the arms and pulled me backward. "What the hell has gotten into you?"

"Shit, Mitch." Cal brought his fingers to his mouth and pulled them away with blood on them. "I just got a job. What the fuck is your problem?"

"It's not like that," I said. My brother still had his arms on me, but I wasn't going to hit him again. "I'm not like that anymore. And Jade is…well, dammit, I love her."

"You love her?" Ian dropped his arms then, and looked at me incredulously. "What did I say? I knew you loved her. It's about time you realized it."

I nodded and dropped my head before I slumped to the floor.

Declan sat down next to me. "You love her? This pregnant mystery woman?"

I nodded again. "I do and I'm afraid I fucked it all up."

I told my brothers everything. All about what an asshole I'd been and how instead of realizing how much I loved her and telling her that, I'd gotten angry and left. They didn't say anything while I was talking. When I was finished, it was Ian who slapped me on my back and helped me to my feet. "Well, it looks like you have some work to do, little brother. But the first thing you're going to do is settle down. No matter what, you cannot go after her guns blazing. You need a plan."

"Agreed," Dec said. "And we'll help. Won't we, guys?"

I looked at each of my brothers in turn, my eyes landing on Cal last. When my youngest brother nodded and smiled, bloody lip and all, I breathed a small sigh of relief. It was a long way from being fixed, but for the first time in days, I felt as if I'd be able to make it okay again. "Thank you."

But the relief was short-lived when the door to the shop opened, Gwen stepped in and pointed directly at me. "You have a lot of explaining to do."

Chapter Fifteen

JADE

TEN MISSED CALLS. At least twice as many text messages. Two voicemails.

All from Mitch.

I held the phone in my hand and tried not to shake. I'd just spent the last few hours talking through everything with Gwen and coming to terms with how I actually felt about Mitch and the baby and everything that was going on.

I couldn't control what Mitch's reaction was to the baby. As Gwen said, there was no doubt he was taken off guard by it all. How could he not be?

Regardless, the only thing I could control in the entire scenario was my reaction to everything, and that was exactly what I was going to do. I was going to control my reaction. And that meant I couldn't let any of his anger in. Not yet. I'd deal with him and his feelings. Of course I would. But for the time being, it hurt too much to know he was angry with me when all I wanted was his arms around me, telling me it would all be okay. Telling me that he loved me.

That's what I really wanted to hear.

I pressed the button to delete the messages without listening to them, and then swiped my fingers to delete the text messages as well.

There would be time for that later, but for the moment, I needed to give myself some time.

Besides, Gwen was right. I could have it all. Maybe that didn't include Mitch, but it *would* include my career and my baby. My mother had been wrong. I could have it all, and I would. But that meant I needed to start by taking charge of something I could control.

I made myself a tea, changed into my comfy clothes and settled into the couch with my laptop to get some work done. I wrote the email I'd been waiting to write all day and hit Send. Not even ten minutes later, my phone rang.

I answered it with a smile. "You love it, don't you?"

"Love it?" Peter's voice boomed over the line. "Absolutely. This is exactly what we wanted. It's exactly what the viewers are going to eat up. It's real, it's raw and it has the makings for a perfect love story."

"I knew you'd love it." I beamed. If Peter was happy with the script, it was going to make my life so much easier. At least when it came to the show. And that's what my focus was. *Control the things I could.*

"Peter, you're absolutely going to love the next few episodes as well," I said. "They get even better. I can send them right now if you like."

"No. I trust you. Wait to send them in the morning. I'm sure that if they're anything like this one, then we'll have a hit on our hands. And with a cast full of up-and-comers, it will be unstoppable."

That's right. I had totally forgotten about the screen test for Bridget. "I assume Bridget did well then?"

"Yes and no."

"What does that mean?" A flicker of unease lit up my stomach. I took a sip of tea and forced myself to remember that I could only control the things that were in my control. At this rate, it was going to become my new mantra. I took a breath. "Is everything okay with Bridget? Or are we looking for a fresh face?"

Secretly, I hoped we could look for a completely undiscovered talent that would take the world by storm. This type of show really needed something special to make it stand out. And although Bridget was good, for a lot of people, she'd always be "that Australian Baywatch star." Never mind the connection to Cal that could get contentious. But I would defer to Peter's judgment if I had to.

"I haven't made up my mind on her yet," Peter said. "Something about delaying her flight to take care of a few things for the season on her current show. And I'll tell you what, Jade, I don't like that. She'll have to fully commit to Mr. Summer if she gets this role. That means she will be Gwen Henderson. No more running around in bathing suits on the beach. This is a serious role, and it will require a full commitment."

"Agreed," I said. "And you're not sure Bridget is up to the job?" I secretly hoped he didn't, although I had no idea why. I had nothing against the woman. In fact, besides a few pictures and magazine articles, and of course the fact that she used to date Cal McCormick, I didn't know anything about her at all. "But I guess we'll just have to wait and see."

"We will. But besides that, it's all coming together. We can begin filming as soon as the last few details are sorted out."

Including the lead actress. I shook my head in wonderment. I didn't know how people who always worked in the industry managed it without going crazy. Working primarily with authors was a much more laid-back job.

"I'll trust you to pull it off, Peter. And in the meantime, I'll keep working with Gwen on the scripts and handling any details on this end."

"You're doing a great job, Jade. Keep it up." Compliments from Peter were rare, and I relished them.

It was still early when I hung up with Peter, but I didn't care. I turned my phone to silent and crawled into bed with a book. The sooner the day was over, the better. Maybe tomorrow I'd be able to handle my life. But there'd be no harm in waiting until then to try.

MITCH

"IT'S GOT TO BE BIG," Gwen said.

We had moved from the Dockside to sitting around a table at the Grizzly Paw, where all of my brothers, with the help of Gwen, were helping me decide what I was going to do to convince Jade I loved her and wanted to be with her and the baby.

After Gwen had returned from her day with Jade and filled me in on the fact that Jade was an absolute mess with the way things were left, and that she'd confided in Gwen how much she loved me and wanted more than anything for me to want to be with her, I knew I had to do something big to fix the mess we'd gotten ourselves into. Clearly there'd been a communication breakdown, but as far as I was concerned, it would be the last time that happened.

I would fix it.

"I'm going to ask her to marry me," I announced to the group. The idea had been formulating since Declan had mentioned his sister-in-laws, but it all crystalized in that moment. And it was a good one. Where even six months ago the very idea of marrying anyone would scare the hell out of me, now, it just felt like the most natural thing I could do.

Because I couldn't imagine my life without her. Not now, not ever.

"Well, I guess a marriage proposal is big." Declan laughed. "It must run in the family, huh?" He gestured with his mug toward Ian, who had proposed to Gwen after their big fight that had almost broken them up forever.

"Maybe so," Ian agreed. "But maybe it's just because we McCormick boys know what we want."

"Or maybe it's because we all screw up our relationships so badly that we need something grand to fix them." Cal shrugged, but I could tell the comment hit home, at least a little, for my younger brother as well.

"So you're really going to ask her to marry you?" Chelsea appeared with a tray of drinks. She'd obviously heard my declaration.

"Do you think that's crazy?"

"Hell no." Chelsea put the drinks down and gave me a quick hug. "But you have to make it big. Don't just ask her. I mean, make sure you're ready."

"Hey." Ian tossed a paper coaster in Chelsea's direction. "Are you saying I didn't do it big enough?"

Ian's proposal to Gwen had been pretty spontaneous, and as far as anyone could tell, totally unplanned. He didn't have a ring or any real intention to do it at all. It had just happened. And that had worked out perfectly for them. But Chelsea was right; for Jade, it needed to be big. She was so uncertain of my love for her that there needed to be no room for doubt. I took a sip of my beer and let an idea percolate.

"Okay." It was Declan who interrupted my train of thought and got right to the point. "So how are you going to do that? You want to marry this woman?"

I nodded. There was no doubt in my mind.

"And you want to be a father to this baby?"

"Absolutely."

"Okay." Declan gave it some thought. "Where are you going to live? Have you given that any thought?"

"It's funny you should ask," I said. "I didn't even have a chance to tell everyone, things have happened so fast—"

"You didn't tell them yet?" Cal shook his head and smiled into his beer.

"Tell us what?" Ian demanded.

"Oh, you don't know." Gwen put her hand to her mouth, looking very guilty, but I just laughed.

"You know?" Ian asked Gwen, who nodded. He turned to me. "Tell me. Now."

I laughed again. "I bought a house."

"No way!" Declan slapped me on the back. "Here? In Cedar Springs?"

I nodded. "Right down the street from the cabin."

"That's great."

It was great. Especially now that it looked as if there would be a family living in that big house.

Don't get ahead of yourself, I chastised myself. First, I needed Jade to see that I loved her and wanted this with her.

But I would. I had no doubt.

Because I couldn't imagine it any other way.

"Wow," Ian said. "I think it is great. Especially since we all seem to be here. We take up a whole lot more space now that we're bigger."

"And there are more of us." Cal waved his hand in Gwen's direction. She smiled and raised her glass in a toast.

"And there will be more in our family soon." I raised my glass as well. "I have to believe that."

"I have no doubt." Gwen clinked glasses with me. "Now, let's get down to details."

"The first thing you need is a ring." All eyes turned to

Declan, who shrugged. "What? You think just because I haven't met the right woman yet, that I don't know a thing or two about romance and doing it right?"

For the next few minutes, we huddled our heads together and came up with a plan. It would involve a lot of work, and more than a little cooperation from some friends in town, but we were all confident it could be pulled off. As far as I was concerned, it had to work. Because the more time that went by without Jade by my side, the more nervous I got that it might never happen.

"IT'S the only place in town that might have one," I said to Declan.

After Chelsea insisted that I couldn't propose without a ring, much debate had ensued as to whether I should go into the city to buy a ring or whether one might be located in Cedar Springs. There was no time to go into the city; besides, there was no way I was going to get that far away from Jade without things being settled between us. The only place I could think of that might have a ring of some kind was the Live, Love, Lake boutique.

I led my brother Declan down Main Street. Of course, Chelsea had wanted to come and help with the ring, but with the dinner hour upon us, the Grizzly Paw was too busy and she needed to work. I promised to text her pictures and let her know when I found one. It was crazy to me how my little sister had become such an important part of my life so quickly. But then again, everything about the summer so far had been unexpected and moving at the speed of light. I might as well just relax into it and enjoy it.

"When did this store open?" Declan asked as we walked up to the door. "It's new, isn't it?" He laughed. "Not that I should be surprised. Everything is new around here. But it's good to be back in town."

"I agree."

"There's just something about Cedar Springs," Dec said. "No matter where I go in the world, it's always been the only place that's ever really felt like home. Is that crazy?"

To anyone else, it might have. But not to me. I knew exactly what my brother was talking about. "Not at all," I said. "I'm glad you're here, Dec. It's important to me that everyone is here for this."

"What about Mom?"

I froze, my hand on the door. *What about Mom?*

Of course I wanted my mother there. But was she ready to come back to the lake? She hadn't been very happy with Ian going to open up the old house. She'd made that clear to me as well when I'd stopped in to see her when school ended. "Did you see her?"

Declan shook his head. "Not yet. I wanted to surprise you all first. But I'll go and get her if you want me to. It's important, Mitch."

I nodded. It was important. "I'd love nothing more than to have her back here with us."

My little brother's smile split his face and he slapped my back. "Consider it done. I'll drive through the night if I have to. But first, let's go see what we can do about a ring."

The bells over the door jingled as we entered and Evie's voice called out from the back. "I'll be right with you."

"Take your time," I responded.

"Who's that?" Declan looked at me with wide eyes when he heard her voice.

I laughed. "That's Evie Rose. She runs the store, and she's just about the sweetest woman you've ever met." It seemed like a million years ago that I thought I might be able to date her. Evie was absolutely a wonderful person, but she was never the woman I needed. It had always been Jade. It was just too bad I hadn't seen it earlier.

Not that it mattered. I would make up for it. I'd spend the rest of my life making up for it.

I wandered to the back of the store where Evie kept a glass case of jewelry and other small items. At first glance, I didn't see what I was looking for, but I had patience.

"Hey, Mitch. Catch."

A child's voice grabbed my attention, and I turned around just in time to see Jonah throw a tennis ball toward Declan, who turned around at exactly the right moment to get hit in the face with it.

"Oops!" Jonah ran through the store to Dec. "You're not Mitch."

Declan rubbed his face. "No," he said good-naturedly. "I'm not. But you have a heck of an arm." He held out his hand for the boy. "I'm Declan, Mitch's brother."

I watched the scene with a chuckle when Evie appeared beside me. "Please tell me Jonah isn't causing trouble out here. I was just putting away some stock in the back and—who is that?" She whispered the question in my ear.

"That's Declan. My younger brother. He just got in from… Well, I can't remember exactly where he was. Out saving the world somewhere." I was just about to call Declan over to introduce him when I saw the look on Evie's face and decided it might be better to do what I came into the store to do before making the introduction. I may not have been the right man for Evie, but judging by the way she was eyeing Dec, there might just be a different McCormick in town who was. "I need your help, Evie. I need a ring."

That got Evie's attention, and I very quickly explained the situation and what it was I needed.

"I think I might just have what you need." Evie clapped her hands. "Wait right here." She disappeared into the back room.

"Does she have something?" Declan appeared at my side, Jonah next to him.

"Hi, Mitch."

"Hey, buddy. Have you been keeping up with your work?" The boy nodded dutifully. "I've tutored him a few times," I explained to Dec. "But he's a smart boy and he didn't need too many sessions before he was more than caught up, did you?"

"That's right," the boy said. "I'm going to be the smartest kid in my class next year. I wish you could be my teacher. It would be so much better than having Mrs. Enderby next year. She's so—"

"That's enough, Jonah." Evie reappeared from the back-room, holding a case in her hand. She shot Declan a shy glance, but still I didn't introduce them. "I think I might have what you need, Mitch."

I followed her over to a little table, and she opened the case to display at least a dozen beautiful antique rings.

"Wow. Evie." I looked up at her in wonder. "These are all so...wow."

"They're all so gorgeous," Declan said beside me. "How will you pick one?"

It was a good question, except for the fact that I already knew exactly what ring I wanted to see on Jade's finger. My hand went instinctually to a ring with a square cut diamond surrounded by smaller diamonds and a simple platinum band. It was perfect for her. Elegant, classic, and brilliant. "This one." I lifted it from the box and held it in front of my eyes.

Yes.

It was the ring. There was no doubt.

"This is the one."

"It's beautiful," Evie said. "It will look amazing on her."

I nodded. "How do you have all these? And why are they in the back? I mean, I was only taking a chance that you might have something, or know someone in town who did. I never thought you actually would have such amazing rings."

Evie shook her head and blushed a little. "It sounds so silly, but I have a thing for jewelry, engagement rings specifically. I think it's the romantic in me." I didn't miss the way she looked up at Declan, and her blush deepened. "Anyway, when I started up the store, I really wanted to be able to offer something like this. Maybe I'm crazy, but I think Cedar Springs is one of the most romantic places on earth, and judging by all the relationships that have sprung up around here lately, I don't think I'm the only one."

I nodded in agreement.

"I'll get a proper case built for them, and hopefully all the new love in town will have a place where they can put a ring on it, as my son says."

"I don't say that," Jonah protested. "The girls at school say that." He dropped his head into his hand. "Moms just don't understand anything," he said to Declan. "Will you come play catch with me?"

Declan smiled and looked up at me. Jonah was a compelling kid, that was for sure. And there was no doubt that Dec would love to go play catch with him, but I knew I could count on him. "I'd love to," Dec said to the boy. "But I promised my brother I'd help him out with some stuff tonight. Maybe we could play sometime soon, though?" Jonah nodded. He turned to focus on Jonah's mother. "I'm Declan, by the way. I can see my brother is probably not going to introduce us."

"Evie." She held out her hand, and Dec turned it and kissed the top of it. If anyone else did it, it might have seemed cliché. But Declan was a class act, and on him, it looked natural. Judging by Evie's reaction, she agreed.

"Evie, we must have met when we were kids," Declan said. She nodded, because there was no doubt their paths had crossed at some point. "But I'm glad to properly make your acquaintance."

I sighed. If the two of them wanted to be Cedar Springs' latest love match, that was fine by me, but they'd have to wait because I had a lot to do and not a lot of time to do it in and I had no problem being selfish in this regard. "Now that you've officially met, don't you have something very important to do for me?"

Declan laughed and said his good-byes, leaving me to finish up my purchase.

Before I left, I told Evie the rest of my plans and she demanded to be allowed to help. As the owner of a boutique and someone who clearly believed in love, Evie had some great ideas and I more than welcomed them. By the time I left to carry out the rest of my plan, I was a little more excited but even more nervous with what I was about to do. But the nerves were good. I was going to need them to get through the night.

Chapter Sixteen

JADE

IT WAS A NEW DAY. The sun was shining, I'd had almost twelve hours of solid sleep, and I was ready to face the day. And my life. I walked into Dream Puffs, as had become my morning routine, placed an order for a peppermint tea and a blueberry muffin and had settled into a table with my laptop, all with a smile on my face. If it was one thing I had learned early on, it was to fake it till you make it. Normally it was applied to my career, but in this instance it was going to work for my personal life as well.

I didn't really have any other choice.

"Good morning." I looked up from my muffin to see Deanna Gordon standing next to my table with a coffee in hand. "Do you mind if I sit?"

"Not at all." I waved to the empty seat and she settled in.

"I'm sure you have work to do," Deanna apologized. "But I saw you here and I thought I should check in with you. It's been a few days since you got the news and I know how something like that can be...well, I guess I don't really know. But

I've seen enough patients looking every bit as shocked as you were to have an idea of what it must feel like." She smiled warmly.

She really was a likeable person and I pictured us being friends one day. The thought surprised me a little. I'd never really had friends. Not real ones anyway. But maybe in a town like Cedar Springs such a thing would finally be possible.

"Thank you," I said. "I'm actually doing really well." I stopped and shook my head. "No. That's a lie." There was no point hiding the truth. "I've actually really been struggling," I answered honestly. "The last few days have been hard. I told everyone involved the news."

"Mitch?"

I nodded, forgetting for a moment that in a small town, everyone knew everything about everyone, so I couldn't hide anything anyway.

"And how did he take it?"

I forced myself to keep the smile on my face. "Well, I think he was more than a little taken off guard."

Deanna reached out and squeezed my hand. "I'm sure he was. But don't worry. I have a feeling everything will turn out just fine. Gwen may have let it slip that you were thinking of staying in town after the show was done shooting?"

I laughed and nodded. "I am. I think it seems like a great place to raise a child, and I have to be honest with you, I've never in a million years thought that I would want a family of any kind or this kind of life at all."

"And now?"

"Now I think it's exactly what I want." I took a slow, thoughtful sip of my tea. "It's kind of a funny feeling when everything I was ever raised to believe I wanted turns out to be the exact opposite of what I want. But I think I'll do things a little differently." I put my hand on my still flat stomach and made a silent promise to my unborn baby to let him or her make their own decisions.

"I think our parents do the very best they can with the information they have at the time." Deanna's smile was so kind, it almost made me cry. I'd done more crying in the last few days than in my entire life. "But I know you're going to be a fantastic mother. And I'm excited for you to be staying." Deanna sat up abruptly, her face lit up with excitement. "In fact, I know the perfect house for you. It's on the lake and close enough to town to be around everything, but far enough away to have some privacy. It's amazing. You have to see it."

The switch in topic took me off guard. "I don't know, Dea—"

"I will not take no for an answer." She jumped up from her chair. "I'll tell you what. Meet me back here at four. Please?"

The last thing I wanted to do was look at a house for sale. I was not in the market for a house in Cedar Springs. Not yet. I had way too many things to worry about; I didn't need to worry about buying a house, too. But on the other hand, I did want to do my best to forge new friendships and Deanna was just trying to be friendly. I sighed and smiled.

"I'll tell you what," I said. "I'll meet you later if maybe we can grab a bite to eat after." It was a good compromise. Besides, I needed to eat and if we could develop our friendship a little further in the process, that could only be a good thing.

"Absolutely." Deanna gave me a big hug. "I'll see you at four and I promise you will not be disappointed." And just like that, she was gone.

I had to laugh. I'd never seen anyone so excited about showing me an empty house before. It was the least I could do to go look at it. Besides, I couldn't rent forever and maybe putting down roots of my own would help take my mind off Mitch.

MITCH

EVERYTHING WAS READY. Everything was perfect.

My brothers, our friends, and I had worked through the night setting everything up and it was just...perfect.

I stood in the doorway, surveying our handiwork, and shook my head in wonder for at least the dozenth time that day. "It's perfect," I said to Cal and then laughed at myself. "I can't seem to find any other word to use."

"That's because there is no other word," Cal agreed. "It is perfect. She's going to love it."

"How do you know?"

"Because how could she not?"

I nodded. *Exactly.* How could she not?

"It was pretty amazing of Milena to get the previous owner to let you in early," Cal said. "How did she manage that?"

I didn't know how she'd managed it, but as soon as I got the idea to hold my surprise at the new house, what I hoped would be our house, I'd gone straight to Milena and she'd made it happen.

"I don't really know," I answered honestly. "But I owe her one. This was my plan A and to be totally honest, my only plan."

"She's pretty amazing."

There was something in Cal's voice that made me turn and stare at him. I was pretty sure we weren't talking about Jade anymore. Was my little brother smitten with the cute, curvy real estate agent? The distraction from my own issues was welcome as I entertained the thought.

Cal had never been the ladies' man type. Despite a career being surrounded by beautiful women all the time, he had always been a one-woman man. He'd only had a few serious girlfriends over the years, at least that the others knew about, but I was pretty sure that was because there had only been those few. Largely that was due to the fact that my little brother was very picky when it came to women. So for him to be even a little bit interested in a woman was big news.

"Have you had a chance to talk more with Milena?" I asked him.

Cal shook his head. "Not much, no. There's a lot going on right now. I want to make sure you get everything done before Jade shows up." He turned back to me and grinned. "There'll be time later. I did ask her to stick around. I hope that's okay."

I laughed. "Why not?"

When I first started thinking of asking Jade to marry me, it was going to be a small, intimate moment. Just the two of us. But Chelsea was right: it had to be big. And the more we brainstormed, the bigger the idea got.

The second Milena got me the keys to the house, Gwen and Chelsea—when she got off work—got busy cleaning and decorating. They'd worked through the night and it showed. The place was gorgeous. Fresh flowers filled every available space and candles and twinkling lights were prepared to be lit as soon as the sun faded from the sky. A trail of daisy petals led through the house to the large covered deck, which was where I'd be standing waiting for her the moment she arrived.

I felt the ring in my pocket.

Everything was ready. I'd managed to rein in the women enough to keep the entire town from getting wind of my plans, but I was starting to get nervous that she wouldn't show up. She had to show up. Everything else was ready.

Cold beads of sweat broke out on my brow and I couldn't stand still a moment longer.

"Hey." Cal's arm stopped me from walking away. "Are you okay? You don't look so good."

Vaguely, I heard Cal call for Ian, and before I knew it, my brothers were leading me outside.

"You're okay." Ian pushed me down into a chair. The fresh breeze blowing off the lake cooled me, and I immediately felt better.

I nodded. "I am."

"Holy shit." Cal leaned against the deck rail across from me. "I thought for sure you were going to pass out."

"Here." Dec appeared and shoved a glass of water in my hand. "Drink this."

I did as I was told, only barely registering the fact that Declan was back from his errand and I had no idea if he'd been successful.

"Are you feeling better?" Ian asked.

I nodded. "I am. I don't know what came over me. One minute I was fine and then…"

"You realized you're about to make the biggest decision of your life."

I nodded again. "Yeah. But that's not what I'm worried about."

"What then?" Declan asked.

I took a deep breath and put words to my worry. "What if she says no?" Just saying the words out loud filled me with dread. What if she did say no?

We were all silent for a few minutes, which I appreciated more than the empty words that would have only been telling me what I wanted to hear. Having my brothers' companion-ship meant more than anything else could have.

"Thanks, guys," I said after my heart rate returned to normal and I was once again able to think clearly. "I appre-ciate you all being here more than you could know."

"It is pretty cool," Cal said. "All of us here together."

"Kind of like old times," Declan added.

"Only better this time." Ian put his arms around his little

brother's, and I stood to join them. "It's nice to be all together."

"Well…" I looked to Declan. "Are we all together?"

Declan nodded. He'd been successful in fetching our mother. "Mom's resting at the house," he confirmed. "I'm just about to go get her."

"Mom's here?" Ian's eyes were wide. "You really are the magical brother, aren't you?"

"Hardly." Declan laughed. "But it was time. She's ready to meet Chelsea. It's just too bad Amber isn't here."

"Soon enough," Cal said. "She needs to finish her internship first, or whatever it is she's doing. Her focus is on her career, and Amber is nothing if not focused."

I spent another minute soaking in my brother's companionship, before I broke free. "Okay, I'm ready to do this. I think I might go crazy if I have to wait another day without seeing her."

"Just another few hours, brother." Ian slapped me on my back. "Gwen called and confirmed Deanna will pick her up at four. They'll be here twenty minutes after that, and then it's all you. Can you handle it?"

I nodded. There was no doubt in my mind that the minute I saw her, I'd find the right words to tell her exactly how I felt.

Hopefully, she'd feel the same way.

Chapter Seventeen

JADE

BY THE TIME four o'clock rolled around, the last thing I wanted to do was meet Deanna to go look at a house. The only thing I really wanted to do was have a hot bath and another early night.

Maybe I could live the next few months by working all day and crashing early so I didn't have to deal with anything else. But I knew I couldn't do that; besides, I did want to foster friendships, so I freshened up, put on one of my new sundresses and dutifully met Deanna in front of the bakery right on time.

"You look so cute." Deanna pulled me in for a quick hug and a kiss on the cheek. "That's a great dress!"

I smiled. "I got it at Evie's new store. She's a miracle worker, helping me pick out so many clothes that actually look good on me."

"Hardly." Deanna laughed. Together we walked down the street to where her car was parked. "You'd look good in anything with that body. Seriously, girl. I'd die to wear something like that."

"You're gorgeous." I meant it. Deanna was curvy in all the right places. "Don't be ridiculous."

"Isn't it true that we always want what we don't have?" She laughed. "But that's okay. Marcus likes all my curves, just fine." She winked and we laughed. For a minute, it felt as though I did have a real girlfriend, and it felt good. I was glad I'd made the decision not to cancel.

"Well, for what it's worth," I said. "I don't think this dress will fit in a few months." I ran my hands over my stomach. It was still flat, of course, but there was definitely a thickening starting. It wouldn't be long before I'd need new clothes again. "I wonder if Evie carries maternity clothes?"

"She should!" Deanna laughed. "This town is blowing up with pregnancies or people I anticipate to see in my office soon, if you know what I mean." She wiggled her eyebrows and laughed again. "Come on. I can't wait to show you this house." She looped her arm through mine and together we all but skipped down the street to the car.

"I really don't know if I need a house right now, Deanna." We were driving out of town toward the house that Deanna was so positive I would like.

"Please." She smiled brightly. "Call me Dee. All my friends do."

Her words gave me a warm feeling inside. *Friends.*

With every day that passed, I was more and more certain that my mother had been wrong. Maybe about everything. Friends and family were important. I should want them. And now I would. Gwen and Deanna. Two friends. It was more than I'd ever had before. A twinge of regret hit me as Mitch's face popped into my head.

At least I'd have the friends part.

"Okay, Dee." I forced myself to be in the moment. "But I really don't think I need a house."

"Of course you do. Your baby will need a nursery. A proper place to call home. Not just a rental house tucked on a busy road behind Main Street. You need a home, Jade. Every family needs a home."

"Ha!" I couldn't help myself. "I need a family first before I need a home."

Dee slowed the car and looked over at me. "I know this isn't happening the way you expected," she said kindly. "And maybe it's not my place to say, but I think the best thing you can do now is have an open mind to everything. I mean, you didn't think things would happen the way they have up until this point, right?"

"No." I shook my head. "Definitely not."

"Right. But the baby is a good thing."

My hand went to my stomach and without hesitation, I said, "It absolutely is. I never would have thought it would be, but now I see that life has a funny way of working out just the way it should."

"Exactly!" Deanna declared. "Remember that, too. Because sometimes an opportunity comes, only for a moment, and then it's gone. You have to take it while you can."

I gave my new friend a strange look, but nodded because even in her strange way, what Dee was saying was true. Sometimes there was only a moment.

I let myself think about that for a second. About how maybe my love with Mitch was only for a moment, if it had been love at all, and how I'd actually been happy, even if it was only for a moment. I could have let myself think about that idea for a long time except all of a sudden, Dee was pulling the car to a stop beside a beautiful log home.

"We're here," she said. "Isn't it perfect?"

I stared out the window. It was perfect. For a family. It was most definitely not the perfect house for a single mom who was about to move her entire life to a new town and start over. A small bungalow right in the heart of town would be much more suited for that. But for the right family, there was no doubt, the house I was staring at would be ideal.

"It's amazing," I answered, unwilling to disappoint my friend.

"Come on. You have to see what's inside."

I opened the door and followed Deanna up the driveway. "Shouldn't there be a real estate agent meeting us? Do you have a key?"

"I don't need a key." Deanna was practically giddy with excitement. "Oh." She stopped short right outside the door. "I just realized I left something in the car. You go on ahead, okay? I'll be right there."

"I'll wait."

"No. You have to see the view when you walk in. You can see through the entire house and look right out to the big deck and the lake behind. It's the most perfect view you'll ever see." Deanna hesitated and dropped her hand. "*Trust* me!"

She looked adamant, and it's not as though I were going to buy the house anyway. The whole thing was just about humoring my friend. With a sigh, I turned, opened the door and my heart stopped for a moment.

There were flowers everywhere, candles flickered, and twinkly white lights strung all over made it look like there were stars inside. It was breathtaking and magical and not at all what an open house should look like.

I took a step back and turned to look for Deanna. Her car, and she, were gone.

I turned back to the house. My heart raced in my chest. And that's when I saw it. The view Dee had spoken of. The one I was supposed to see when I first walked through the front door.

Just like she had promised, I could see straight through the room, out to the deck, the lake, and...

Mitch.

MITCH

I HAD NEVER BEEN SO nervous.

My legs shook, my heart raced, and despite the warmth of the evening, cold droplets of sweat trailed down my spine. My hand went into my pocket, my fingers wrapped around the ring I had there and instantly my breathing slowed.

It would all work out.

I watched, unspeaking, as she stepped into the house, looked around in wonder and turned to leave. She stopped.

Good, that must mean that Deanna had left quickly. Damn. I owed her one for her part in my plan. She turned around again. This time she looked straight through the house toward the lake. And me.

I smiled.

She still didn't move.

I wanted to call out to her, to yell and ask her to come talk to me, but my voice wouldn't work, so I did the only thing I could think of that would get her attention.

I got down on one knee.

Even from across the room, I could see the shock on her face. I kept the smile on mine, willing her to walk toward me so she could see for herself the love in my eyes. The love I'd felt all along but was just too stupid to admit.

It felt like a million years went by but finally she started to walk through the flower-filled living room and out to the deck. There were more flowers out here, and even more lights that would look amazing when the sun fully disappeared. But for the moment, I was glad it was still light out so she could see me clearly.

"Mitch?" Her voice shook in question when she stepped outside. "Mitch, what are you—"

I held out my hand, silencing her questions.

She didn't have to, and after the way I'd behaved I wouldn't have blamed her if she didn't, but she took my hand.

"Mitch, I—"

"Please," I interrupted her. "I'm sure you have so much to say and so many questions for me and maybe even you want to yell at me a little bit." That earned me a smile. "And I want to give you the chance to do all of that. But first I really need to say something. Will you let me have that chance?"

She nodded and it took all my self-control to keep from jumping up, pulling her into my arms and kissing her. She was so amazingly beautiful and her willingness to give me a chance made her even more stunning. My heart swelled.

"Jade, I have been the biggest idiot," I started. "From the minute I met you at the summer solstice festival, I knew there was something amazing about you. You're gorgeous, strong, witty, smart, and successful. I was speechless. And the connection we had, it was electric and instant. And maybe that's why I didn't realize right away that it could possibly be real. I mean, how could it be possible to fall in love the moment you met someone?"

Her eyes filled with tears. It stopped me. I'd never seen her cry before. Was she a crier? Or did she hold everything in? There was still so much I didn't know about her. Still so much I had to discover. The idea excited me.

I squeezed her hands a little tighter in my own and continued. "I was convinced that it couldn't be true, that what we had couldn't possibly be what I thought it was. But I was wrong. It's everything."

"Mitch, I—"

"No. Jade, it is. And I wanted to tell you that earlier but then you told me about the baby and how you didn't want or expect anything from me and well…it hurt. And yes, of course you surprised me with that. I mean, I didn't expect to hear that I was going to be a father."

She laughed and wiped at her eyes. "I certainly didn't expect to tell you that."

"But I'm so sorry about the way I handled it. I never should have gotten upset like that. I never should have—"

"No," she interrupted me. "I never should have been so cold." She crouched down so we were eye to eye. "I just thought…well…I just thought you weren't interested in being with me, and I didn't want you to feel you had to be. I never want anyone who doesn't want—"

I silenced her with a kiss. "I want you, Jade. Make no mistake about it. I want you and our baby and…everything."

She closed her eyes and shook her head gently.

"Yes." I took her chin in my hand. "I love you. Look at me." She did as I requested. "I love you," I said again, slower. "And I want to be with you. Do you believe me?"

For a moment, she didn't do or say anything. I held my breath and finally she nodded. "Yes."

I pulled her face into my hands again and kissed her thoroughly.

"You believe me?" I asked again and stood, taking her with me. "I really need you to believe that despite everything, I love you. And I know it's fast, and I know it's crazy, but when I'm with you I feel like I've never felt before. When I'm holding you, I feel like I'm home. Like there's no place else I'd rather be than in your arms, and I—"

"I believe you." Her eyes danced with laughter and tears, but it was the smile on her face that gave me the answer I needed. She did believe me. "And it's the craziest thing, but I love you, too. So much."

I kissed her again. My arms wrapped around her, holding her tight while my lips pressed against hers, taking love as much as I gave it. I was so lost in her that I almost forgot what I needed to do. I regained my senses and pulled back, once more dropping to one knee. This time, I reached into my pocket and pulled out the ring.

"Mitch, what are you…get up…"

I shook my head. "Jade, it took me longer than it should have, but my eyes are completely open now. I love you, and I want to spend the rest of my life falling deeper in love with you." I held out the ring. "Will you do me the great honor of being my wife?"

She didn't even hesitate. "Yes." She nodded her head. "Yes. Oh, God. A thousand times yes."

I slipped the ring on her left hand and kissed it before I stood and pulled her into my arms. "I'm so glad you said yes," I murmured into her hair.

She pulled back slightly and looked me in the eyes. "How could I say anything else? Just like you, I fought all of this. The way I felt about you scared me, Mitch. I reasoned it away to be anything but love. But now…well…now I believe. And to hear you say you feel the same way…" Tears spilled over her cheeks and she swiped at them with a laugh. "I can't seem to stop crying."

"It's okay."

"I know." She smiled. "I know it is. And I can't believe I'm going to say this but, I can't wait to marry you and be a family with you."

I knew how crazy that was for her to say given everything she'd told me about her childhood and what she'd been raised to believe. "I'm so glad to hear you say that." I grinned. "Because I'm not done with the surprises. Turn around."

JADE

AFTER MITCH'S confession of love, I probably would have done anything he asked, I was flying so high. It couldn't get any better than to hear that he felt the same way I did.

But then it did get better.

Because I turned around.

Just inside, in the very living room full of flowers I'd just walked through, stood all our family and friends. They all held a single flower in their hands, and wore the biggest smiles I had ever seen.

Confused, I turned to Mitch. "What is this?"

He took my left hand and held it to his lips before he wrapped it in his. "This is our wedding."

Speechless, he led me through the door and we were greeted by cheers and celebration before each of our friends and family members came up to us one by one to offer their congratulations. As each person came up, they handed me the flower they were holding, creating, as they did so, a beautiful bouquet.

Deanna stepped up and handed me a lily and gave me a hug. I looked between my new friend and my new fiancé—that was going to take some getting used to, saying—a look of confusion on my face. "How did you...were you...weren't you..."

Deanna laughed. "Oh, sweetie. We had to get you here somehow, didn't we?" She kissed me on the cheek. "But this was all Mitch's idea. He planned everything."

"With a lot of help from everyone else."

Deanna moved off. The next person, a woman, grabbed my hand and handed me a rose with the other one. "Jade." She squeezed. "I can't tell you how happy I am to meet the woman who holds my son's heart."

Son.

"Mrs. McCormick?"

"Please. Call me Maureen."

There was something about the woman, her smile, the fact that she was Mitch's mother, and she was there and—I pulled her in for a spontaneous hug. "It's so nice to meet you."

Maureen laughed. "It's a pleasure to meet you too, sweetie. And I can't wait to get to know you better, but I think my son has a few ideas about how the rest of this evening should go." She turned and gave her son a hug, whispering into his ear, but not so quiet that I couldn't hear. "I like her, Mitch. I love you, son."

I waited until she wandered away, and before the next person came to deliver me a flower, I turned to Mitch. "I still don't understand. What is all this?" I gestured to the people who'd gathered in the large room. "What did you mean it's our wedding?"

"Just that." He took my hand and led me a few steps away. "I don't want to wait, Jade. I want to be with you and not just as my fiancée. As my wife. And I think you want that too. Let's be a family."

He put his hand on my stomach and gave me the sweetest smile. It was the first time he'd done that. The first time he'd acknowledged, really acknowledged that we could be a family.

But it was so soon.

Did that matter? Did it matter that we'd only known each other six weeks and already we were having a baby and getting married?

Of course it mattered!

It was crazy. Who did that? Nobody did that. Because it was insane.

I looked down at where his hand was still on my stomach. I placed mine on top of his, my new diamond ring sparkling up at me. We both looked up into each other's eyes at the same time. I could see the love in his eyes. It radiated out from him and hit me with its warmth.

"Yes." I nodded. "I do. I want nothing more than to be a family with you. And yes, it's crazy." I closed my eyes and laughed a little, hoping I didn't sound too maniacal. "It's so freakin' crazy, but that's why I know it's going to work. This is right. This is so right. I do want to marry you. I do."

He laughed and placed a finger on my lips. "Save it for the ceremony, babe." He replaced his finger with his lips and kissed me sweetly.

"But how?" I asked. "How did you do all this? How can we get married today? Is everyone here?"

"Who do you want here?"

My mother. I should have my mother there. After all, she was the only family I had. She should be in attendance, shouldn't she? But no. My mom would ruin everything. She'd tell me I was making a mistake and never to sign my life away for a man and a child. But my mom didn't know Mitch. She didn't know this love. She couldn't have. There was no way that if my mother had ever felt a love like I was feeling, she would ever have been able to coach me to avoid it. No. My mom didn't belong here. Not today. I'd talk to her later, definitely. But that day was not today.

I looked around the group that was gathered. All of Mitch's brothers. Including one I assumed to be Declan but hadn't actually met yet. The family resemblance was so uncanny it couldn't be anyone but. Gwen was there, of course, and Deanna. Evie and her son, Jonah. A handful of people I didn't know yet, but assumed were important to Mitch. I looked back at my fiancé.

"I have everyone I need."

"Are you sure? Because we can—"

"I'm sure." I nodded, never feeling more confident about a decision in my life. Being with Mitch felt right. It was what I wanted. It's what I'd wanted from the very beginning. And it might be the most ridiculous thing I'd ever done, but I needed to take a leap of faith, stop second-guessing my heart, put aside all of the objections I'd had drilled into my head my entire life, and do what felt right. "Let's do this."

He squeezed my hands tighter and kissed them. "There's just one more thing." He looked over his shoulder and beckoned to Evie, who a moment later was at my side.

"Come with me, Jade." She took my hand from Mitch's. "We have to get you ready."

I still had so many questions, but they could all wait because the only thing that was important was Mitch, my baby, and becoming a family.

———

THIRTY MINUTES LATER, dressed in the prettiest ivory lace dress I'd ever seen, with the bouquet of flowers from our guests in my hand, I was ready to walk down the aisle. I stood trembling in the doorway of one of the bedrooms. When the hauntingly beautiful guitar sounds started, I walked down the hallway and back into the great room that was now lit up by the candles and twinkle lights that had been strung around the room. I didn't even notice the faces of the people I passed, or the fact that the man playing the guitar was none other than the world-renowned musician, Slade Black.

I only had eyes for Mitch, who stood by himself next to Pastor Christopher.

When Evie was helping me get dressed, she filled me in on some of the details such as the pastor, who'd been secured at short notice because he was an old friend of the family's. Everything else Evie had told me was a blur now. All I could think about was becoming Mitch's wife and how right it felt.

Somehow I made it to the front of the room. Mitch took my hand and steadied me. I hadn't even realized I was shaking.

"Are you okay, babe?"

I nodded. "More than okay." He kissed me lightly on the cheek and I laughed. "Is this crazy?"

"The only thing that's crazy is how we didn't realize our love sooner."

"Well, we're both pretty stubborn."

He kissed my forehead and I didn't think I would ever get enough of him kissing me. "One of my favorite things about you."

"If you're both ready," Pastor Christopher interrupted us. "We will begin." We nodded and turned to the pastor. He began the ceremony, most of which I couldn't remember. That is, until it came to the vows. "Do you vow to honor and cherish Mitch as your husband and partner as long as you both shall live?"

I didn't even hesitate. "I absolutely do."

He grinned at me. "And do you, Mitch, vow to honor and cherish Jade as your wife and partner as long as you both shall live?"

He looked straight in my eyes and with conviction, said, "Oh hell yeah." He clapped a hand to his mouth when he realized what he'd said but everyone, including Pastor Christopher, laughed. "I mean," he straightened up and tried again, "I do."

With a chuckle, and probably a roll of his eyes, the pastor declared us husband and wife. Mitch wrapped me in his arms, dipped me low and kissed me so thoroughly, we might have been the only ones in the room.

A cheer went up among our friends and family. We turned to face the gathered group and the pastor announced us for the first time. "I give you, Mr. and Mrs. McCormick."

The cheer grew louder, but I turned to Mitch and said, "I think I might keep my last name. At least professionally."

He laughed and squeezed my hand. "I wouldn't have it any other way, babe."

Happiness and warmth filled me. This man was absolutely perfect. And he was mine.

Chapter Eighteen

MITCH

I COULD HAPPILY HAVE SLEPT all day with my wife in my arms. However, my new bride was an early riser and when I woke, keenly aware that she was no longer in my arms, I tugged on a pair of shorts and went in search of her.

The living room of our new home was a mess from the night before. We'd feasted on the delicious food Jax Carver from the Springs restaurant had created for us, danced the night away to Slade Black's music, and when he wanted to join in, to some playlists that had been created, and finally, when I couldn't stand one more minute, I kicked everyone out so I could be alone with my wife. Cleanup hadn't seemed as important as taking my bride to bed.

As far as I was concerned, the mess could keep waiting.

Jade sat on the deck, wrapped in a blanket from the bed, her hands wrapped around her knees. I moved up behind her and kissed her neck. "Good morning, Mrs. McCormick."

She turned to me and kissed my lips. "Mmm. I do like the sound of that."

"So do I," I said. "A lot." I sat down in the chair next to her and took her hand.

We sat in silence for a few minutes, before I asked, "How are you feeling this morning? About everything."

"So good." She turned in her chair and grabbed my other hand. "I don't think I've ever been happier. And this place, this view." She turned out to the lake again. "It's amazing. But I have a question for you."

"Anything."

"This house...Deanna said it was for sale and I know you bought one the other day. But...can we..."

My smile split my face. "It's ours. I closed on it a few days ago and then Milena sweet-talked the previous owner into letting me have a super-fast possession."

"What? This is the house you bought?"

I nodded. "It's one of those things that just kind of fell into place. And I knew the second I saw the house that I wanted to be here with you. And it's the perfect place for a family, don't you think?"

She nodded. "I do." Jade laughed. "I feel like I've been saying that a lot lately."

I moved so I was out of the chair and in front of her. I held both her hands in mine and looked straight into her eyes. "I hope you say that every day for the rest of your life, babe. Because I intend to spend the rest of my days making you happier than you've ever been and I can't wait to give you the family you never had."

I pulled her into my arms and held her. I could hardly believe my luck. Not only had I found the perfect woman for me, despite my best efforts to screw it up, I'd married her. Life couldn't get any better.

"I wish I could give you a honeymoon," I said a few minutes later. "But Gwen said something about the show and how you were going to start filming soon, plus I need to make arrangements with Principal Crane. I heard there might be an opening at the school for me."

"Really?"

I nodded. "You do agree that Cedar Springs is the perfect place to raise a family, don't you?" There was so much we still had to talk about. Fortunately, we had the rest of our lives to sort out the details.

"Absolutely." She smiled, full of contentment, and turned to look out at the lake again. "It's just beautiful here and peaceful. You were so lucky to have spent summers out here. And how great that all your brothers and your mom were here."

I felt a flicker of guilt. "I'm sorry your mom wasn't here."

"No." Her mouth pressed into a thin line. "I'm not. It wouldn't have been right. Not last night. But soon, okay? I want you to meet her, and I want her to come here and see our love and that it can be different than what she experienced. You never know—maybe she'll finally have her own happy ending."

"It could happen." I reached for her hand again. "As soon as you want, we'll have her here. In our home."

She squeezed my hand. "I like the sound of that. Our home. One more thing, Mitch?"

"Anything, babe."

She stood, and I joined her at the deck rail. "Right there." I followed her hand to where she pointed down to the lake. "We need a dock and a boat of our own."

"A boat?"

There was a wicked glint in her eye. "Definitely. Just because we're married now it doesn't mean that our little boat rendezvouses will end, does it?"

Damn. I was a lucky man.

I reached for Jade, pulling her in for a deep kiss full of promise of what would come. "I promise you, babe. Even when we have five little kids running around, those will never end."

"Five?" She pulled back, a look of shock on her face.

"Oh, at least five," I joked. "I plan on keeping you very busy. In fact, I think we should get started right now."

It was her turn to laugh. She swatted me playfully. "We already did get started, remember?"

My hands went protectively to her belly. I bent and gave it a gentle kiss, before giving her a much more passionate one. "Then, I think we should get a bit more practice in, don't you?"

Before she could answer, I scooped her up easily in my arms and carried my wife over the threshold and into our new house.

Looking for a little more Jade and Mitch? I have an exclusive bonus scene just for you! And as an extra bonus, this scen includes a few photos, so you can see for yourself the beautiful location of Cedar Springs! Click here to get that exclusive scene.

Next...
It's baby brother, Cal's turn to fall in love next in One more Moment. But will love have a chance to shine in the spotlight?

And if you want even more romance...click HERE for an exclusive FREE novella that isn't available anywhere else!

One More Moment

**Please enjoy an excerpt from the next in the series -
One More Moment**

MELINA

THERE WEREN'T many summer days in Cedar Springs that weren't absolutely gorgeous. By and large, the small mountain town was blessed with hot summer days and warm nights, perfect for sitting around the campfire.

But even in a perfect summer town, it had to rain sometimes. But as far as I was concerned, it did not have to rain on the first day I wanted to try paddleboard yoga. I dropped my curtains with a sigh and turned away from the window. The clouds were socked in through the valley; it wasn't going to stop raining anytime soon. I might as well come up with an alternative plan.

"Good morning, Dad." I made my way into the small

kitchen where my dad was having his morning coffee and working on his daily crossword puzzle.

"Hardly," he grumbled. "I don't know what's so good about it. This weather has put a damp in my bones and my arthritis is acting up. But if you think it's so good, I guess there must be something to say about it."

I laughed and gave my dad a kiss on the cheek. "The way you carry on I would think that you were eighty, Dad. It's just a little bit of rain. It'll be all cleared up by tomorrow, I'm sure."

Despite the fact that my dad was a big grouch, I knew he was all bark and no bite. I'd spent most of my life dealing with his moods, and over the years I'd realized his Oscar the Grouch act was just that—an act.

Either way, he'd forced me to be a cheerier person in an effort to balance the scales. It was a relationship that worked. Especially now that it was just the two of us again.

A shudder ran through me at the memory. It wasn't that long ago when there had been an even more negative influence in my life. And a real negative influence, not just a grumpy old man complaining about the weather.

My ex-boyfriend, Michael Malone, had almost ruined me with his backhanded comments, subtle putdowns, not-so-subtle insults, and general belittling. Yes, he'd almost ruined me. But I was strong. It would take a lot more than an insecure man with a host of issues of his own to destroy me.

It hadn't been easy, but I'd made the changes I needed to get out from under him and end our relationship.

It was definitely good to be back to just the two of us again. I looked over at my dad, who grumbled something to himself about the crossword puzzle.

No doubt he disagreed with one of the answers. He always thought he knew better than the newspaper. I smiled and chuckled a little. I would take my father's crotchety old attitude any day if it meant never having to deal with a man like Michael Malone again.

"What are you going to do today, Dad?" I poured myself a cup of coffee, skipping the milk and sugar, and leaned against the counter. "It's Saturday—you must have something fun planned."

I tried not to laugh because although there was no doubt my dad had something planned, fun wouldn't likely be the word I'd use to describe it. No doubt he had some sort of chore lined up, or maybe a fishing trip. Either way, it definitely wouldn't be my idea of fun.

"Well, I was going to go see if the fish were biting. But with this weather, I guess that's off. There's no reason that it can't rain during the week, but no... The minute Saturday rolls around, Mother Nature needs to spit in your face. So I guess I'll just go out to the shed, see what needs fixing."

I couldn't help myself anymore. The laughter that had been threatening burbled out. My dad was just so damn predictable.

"What are you laughing at?"

I shook my head and bit my lip, but the laughter wouldn't stop. Especially when I caught my dad try to hide his own grin behind his coffee mug.

"Okay, I get it," he said. "You think you have your old man all figured out. Well, you never know, kiddo. I might just surprise you one day."

I wrapped my dad in a big hug. "I love you just the way you are, Dad. Don't you dare think about changing." I gave him another squeeze and kissed him on the forehead.

My dad reached up and patted my hand, which was his way of saying that he loved me too. He wasn't a man to show his emotions very often, but he didn't need to. I knew he loved me. And although of course it would be nice if I heard it once in a while, I'd take what I could get.

"What are you up to today, Milena?"

I took a sip of my coffee and sighed. I'd meant what I'd said; the rain was probably going to clear up by the end of the day, but it didn't mean it still wasn't ruining my plans for the moment.

"I was going to go try out a new type of yoga on a paddleboard, but with this rain I'll probably just skip it altogether. Besides, I should probably get some work done."

"You work too hard. You should have a little fun," my dad said. "Work can wait. Can't you do your pretzel New Age thing indoors? What exactly is yoga on a paddleboard anyway? That sounds crazy. Isn't a paddleboard one of those old surfboards people paddle around the lake?"

"That's exactly what it is." I shook my head. "And it's supposed to be great for your balance and your core." I tried to explain it to my dad, knowing it was futile.

"Well, even if you can't get out in the rain, you should still go do your yoga New Age pretzel thing. I know how you like it, and it's good for you."

I had to appreciate his concern. Besides, he had a point. I did like it, and it was good for me. And not just my body. My mental state, too. Just because it was raining did not mean I couldn't do yoga. It also didn't mean that I couldn't go find a new environment to do it in instead of my cramped bedroom. And that's just what I was going to do.

"Thanks, Dad. You're right. And you just gave me an idea." It had been just under a year since I dropped fifty extra pounds, plus another two hundred in the form of Michael Malone when I finally got the courage to break up with him and kick him out.

I'd regained my sense of self and self-confidence and had worked damned hard to get my life back. But I needed to stay focused when it came to taking care of myself because there was no way I was going to go back to that dark place again. I couldn't push yoga off just because of the weather. "I'll see you later. Have a fun day in the shed."

I overheard my dad muttering something as I left the room, no doubt about how much fun he would have fixing the old lawn mower, or sharpening a rusty saw and how I had no idea what I was missing. I laughed and went to find my yoga bag. I knew exactly what I was missing.

And I was more than okay with it.

CAL

FOR YEARS, I had done my best to avoid running. I used to like to say that the only way I would be caught running was if something was chasing me, and that something better be a grizzly bear.

Maybe it was because I was back in Cedar Springs, surrounded by the fresh mountain air and the lake breeze after being in the hot Australian sun for so long.

Maybe it was the influence of my sister-in-law to-be, Gwen, who ran a few miles every morning. Whatever it was, in the few weeks since I'd been back in the town I'd spent my childhood summers, I had started to run.

And I liked it.

That morning I'd gotten a later start than I normally did. I usually liked to get out early so I could run along the beach and into town before the tourists started making their way down to enjoy the lake.

But it didn't seem to be a problem on this particular Saturday. The way the valley was clouded up with the rain pouring down, there wouldn't be many people enjoying the beach today. Which was perfect, because my runs were my time to be alone and clear my head.

There were some other perks to my new daily habit, too. Not only did it allow me to eat an extra burger now and then at the local Grizzly Paw pub, I was enjoying getting to know the town again by foot. And as much as I enjoyed the weight room, there was nothing quite like using my own two feet to stay fit.

I'd just landed an amazing breakout role on what could very well be the hottest new television show, Mr. Summer, which happened to be based on my oldest brother, Ian, and his new fiancée, Gwen.

Or more specifically, the show was based on Gwen documenting their entire love story on social media, that almost wasn't a love story at all.

It was kind of strange to know that I was going to be playing my older brother on TV, but it was an amazing opportunity and there was no way I wasn't going to try out for the part. The fact that I'd gotten the role was an awesome surprise.

I had no real acting experience besides a few commercials when I was in Australia. My time there had been spent working as a model and although I'd been very successful doing just that, I was ready for more.

While I was over in Australia, I'd been dating and living with Bridget Murphy, the star of *Beach Bodies*, a Baywatch-type of series set on the beaches of Australia. She was gorgeous and not only did Australia love her, I also had.

At twenty-three, I was the youngest of my four brothers, but that didn't mean I had any interest in waiting to settle down with the right woman. And I'd thought I'd already found that woman. In fact, shortly before I'd left to come back home, I'd been fully prepared to ask her to marry me.

Thank God my eyes had been opened before making that mistake.

I pushed my legs harder through the rain, feeling the sting of the drops on my bare skin as I did. It didn't matter how hard

I ran; I could never seem to outrun the hurt and disappointment that had plagued me since my breakup with Bridget.

When I told her I wanted to go into acting, she seemed so supportive, even to the point of telling me she would help me get some roles.

It wasn't until months of waiting for something to happen with no real progress that I'd discovered the truth. Not only had she not helped me, but she'd actually sabotaged me in the Australian industry. All because she was worried my star might shine brighter than hers.

Immediately after the discovery, I broke up with her, and when I found out about my oldest brother Ian's new show and the opportunity that might be there for me, I got on the next plane home.

Even half a world away, it wasn't enough distance. I needed to get Bridget out of my head and, more specifically, her betrayal. Despite my high-profile career as a model and the constant women who threw themselves at me, I had never been interested in any of those shallow relationships.

I had only ever been interested in settling down with the right woman.

I myself hadn't grown up with the perfect happy family. At least not for half of my life. Far from it. When I was only fourteen, my father announced that he had a secret family, and we had two half-sisters. More to the point, my father had announced he was leaving us for his new family.

For some of my brothers, it had soured them against love, like my older brother Mitch, who had only recently opened his heart to the love of his life, his new wife Jade. But for me, it just made me crave it all the more. I had never given up on the idea that true love existed, and I could have it.

I pumped my arms and pushed down the beach through the rain. I didn't love the rain, but the definite benefit was that

I more or less had the beach to myself. I swiped at the water on my face and kept my stride.

Two of my siblings had found love in Cedar Springs. Maybe it would be lucky for me too. Not that I was really looking. Not now. Mr. Summer started filming soon and I needed to focus on that.

Acting was a whole lot different than modeling, and although I knew I was going to nail the role of my big brother, Ian McCormick, I wanted to make sure I didn't leave anything to chance.

The show was set to be a breakout hit; everyone was talking about it. It could be my big break, so I could finally start doing what I'd always wanted to.

That was my focus.

Career.

Not love.

My stride slowed as I came into town and the public beach area.

The Dockside, my brother's marina, was just on the other side of the beach, with the Grizzly Paw pub just up the road. I'd had thoughts of stopping in to say hi to Ian at the marina, or maybe grab a glass of water from my little sister, Chelsea, who was working the early shift at the Grizzly Paw, but both of those thoughts flew out of my head when I caught sight of the woman under the gazebo.

The gazebo sat in the grassy field just up from the beach. Families liked to picnic there or escape from the hot sun on a nice summer day. I didn't expect to see anyone there now, which was why the sight of a woman stretched out on a blanket took me by surprise.

I slowed my pace until I was walking up to the gazebo steps. A smile crossed my face when I realized I recognized the woman inside. It was Milena Hill, the real estate agent, who helped my brother Mitch buy his new home on the lake just down the street from our family cabin.

Technically, I knew her from when we were kids, and I spent my summers there. But that was a lifetime ago, and we were different people. Besides, I couldn't really remember noticing Milena when we were kids.

But I sure noticed her now.

I stood and watched in the gazebo entrance.

Maybe I shouldn't have, but I expected her to open her eyes at any minute, so it wasn't really as if I was eavesdropping or intruding on a private moment. At least that's how I justified it to myself.

The truth was, I'd been hoping to run into her again. The last time I'd seen her was only a few days earlier at Mitch and Jade's surprise proposal-turned-wedding event.

There was something about this girl. She was so unlike anyone I'd ever spent time with. She wasn't a flashy, glitzy Hollywood type. She was real. And really freaking cute.

My last girlfriend Bridget, had been stick-thin. She'd never eaten much more than a lettuce leaf here or there—at least, that's how it seemed whenever we went out for dinner. But Milena was curvy in all the right places.

This was especially evident with the tight tank top and leggings she wore. Her legs were adorned in bright pink and purple sugar skulls; her top was a basic black tank. It was an interesting choice for lying on her back in the middle of the gazebo, though I couldn't think of any outfit that might be typical for that.

What was she doing?

She still hadn't noticed me. She was lying flat on her back, her arm stretched over her head with her eyes shut. Her lips were pursed and she made a strange sound that sounded like a mix between heavy breathing and chanting.

Yoga?

My question was answered a moment later when she pulled both her legs into her chest, wrapped her arms around them, and did a half roll to a sitting position before she crossed her legs, putting her hands in a prayer position, and bent her head. "Namaste," she whispered to the air.

Definitely yoga.

Not that I had a ton of experience with yoga. Or any at all, really. I'd always kind of thought it was a hippie New Age thing to do, but watching the few moves Milena did was incredibly peaceful and not hippie at all.

But the serenity only lasted a moment because then Milena opened her eyes.

"What the hell?" She sat up so fast her head spun. It took a few seconds before her brain registered that it was me who'd scared the hell out of her.

I held my hands up in front of me. "It's just me," I said, trying not to smile. "I didn't mean to startle you."

"Were you watching me?" When she realized she wasn't in any danger, her posture softened a little, but she didn't relax entirely. "What the hell, Cal?"

"I was just…I was running…you were…" I took a breath, ran a hand through my overgrown wet hair and tried again. Women didn't fluster me. No woman flustered me. This woman did. "I was out for a run and I saw someone lying down. I thought…well, maybe they were hurt. Anyway, it was you and—"

"So you thought you'd stop and take a look?"

"No," I answered quickly. Too quickly. "I mean, well…yes, I guess."

She crossed her arms over her ample bosom, which had a very desirable effect, and I could see she was trying not to smile when she said, "And?"

"And what?"

Was she flirting with me?

"And, what did you think?"

MELINA

IT WAS A LOADED QUESTION, and I knew it. I couldn't even believe I'd asked him that. If he said that he did in fact like what he saw, I'd know he was interested. But what if he didn't say that? What if he didn't say anything?

Oh God. I could just die.

I never flirted. I never put myself out there. Especially with someone like Cal McCormick.

What was I thinking?

He was amazingly gorgeous, way out of my league and a model, for bloody sake. There was no way he'd ever be interested in me. I was setting myself up for rejection, that's what I was doing.

I took a deep breath and tried to casually adjust my tank top so it didn't cling so much to my stomach. As a general rule, I didn't wear my workout clothes in public, but I hadn't expected to run into anyone.

"I think that it looked very…interesting."

Interesting?

I tried not to react negatively. There could have been worse things he'd said. He could have said that it was ridiculous. That I looked ridiculous in that…*No. Stop it, Milena.* I chastised myself.

I forced myself to stop the negative thinking and instead pasted a smile on my face. "Interesting?" I repeated the word in a way I hoped sounded light and flirty. "Interesting like you would like to try it, interesting? Or interesting as in, what was the crazy woman doing, kind of interesting?"

I might as well make fun of myself a little. I was nothing, if not good at self-deprecation.

He leaned up against the wall of the gazebo. Damn, he looked so casual, so relaxed. And so hot with his tight t-shirt that stuck to his skin from the rain and his shorts that exposed his long, muscular...no.

I could not let myself start thinking of him that way. I forced myself to look into his eyes, but that was just as dangerous. His green eyes sparkled with mischief, and when he finally responded, I just about melted down into a shavasana pose.

"Interesting in the way that I enjoyed watching you do it, but I don't think it's really my thing."

He enjoyed watching?

My heart raced and I was thankful I was already sitting down, because if not, there was no doubt I would have collapsed right there and then.

He'd said he'd enjoyed watching me.

Oh. My. Freakin'. God.

With more composure than I ever thought I'd be able to muster, I nodded and asked him, "Why don't you think you'd like to try? Have you ever done yoga?"

"Yoga!" It was almost comical the way he spat out the word. "No." He chuckled and shook his head. "Yoga isn't my thing. I run."

"You run?"

"And I lift weights."

"Of course you do."

"What does that mean?"

"I mean, it's a really guy thing to do."

He dropped his arms and took a step toward me. "It's an everyone thing to do," he said. "Lots of women lift weights, too. In fact, in my gym in Australia, it was almost fifty percent women."

Australia. Right. It was a sharp reminder of just how out

of my league this guy was. He'd just come from Australia, where he was a famous model. And the only reason he was in Cedar Springs was to star in a new television show.

Yup. It didn't get more out of my league than that.

"Well, we don't have a gym here," I said somewhat defensively.

"You don't really need a gym, you know?" Before I realized what he was doing, he'd jumped up and grabbed onto one of the beams stretched across the rafters.

"What are you—"

"One..." With what looked like remarkable ease, he pulled himself up so his chin touched the top of the beam before he lowered himself. "Two..." He repeated the action. "See? You don't need a gym."

I tried my best not to stare at his biceps. It was a losing battle. It wasn't that he was bulky in a muscle man-bodybuilder type of way, but damn, the man was built pretty perfectly.

And I was fairly sure that if he took his shirt off, there would be at least a six-pack underneath. *At least.*

"I see that." Starting to feel the chill in the air now that my workout was done, I pushed up from the mat and went digging through my bag to find a sweater.

I pulled it quickly over my head, grateful for the layer. "But you can get just as good of a workout doing yoga."

It was something I believed wholeheartedly. I had lost weight and changed my life by practicing yoga five days a week and walking every day.

Of course, I made a point to put healthy foods in my body, but I didn't go crazy and I hadn't used any fancy workout programs or expensive gym memberships or anything else. Yoga and walking. That was it.

"Maybe so." He jumped down and landed in front of me. "But lifting weights is a different type of workout. You should try it."

"I should?" I bent down and rolled up my mat. I couldn't put a finger on it, but something about talking with him in such close proximity made me nervous.

Okay, I could put a finger on it. That was exactly why I was nervous. I was talking to him in close proximity, and he was wearing nothing but a tight and very damp t-shirt.

I looked away, found my water bottle, and took a long sip, pretending to be incredibly thirsty.

"You should," he said again. I probably shouldn't have, but I looked back at him just in time to see his devilish smile. "I think you might like it. I'd be happy to show you sometime."

Had he seriously just said that? Was that like a date? There was no way it was a date. Get a hold of yourself, Milena. He was not asking me on a date.

"That could be fun."

What? I could not even begin to understand why I'd just said that. There was no way I was going to go on a date with him. Especially not one that involved lifting weights, of all things.

"I think it could be very fun." He winked and I tried not to react although my insides had somehow just liquefied.

"And then you can try yoga?" That had come out of nowhere, but once the words were out, I decided to go with it. "I'd be happy to show you a few moves."

I fully expected him to say no. After all, he had already told me he wasn't the yoga type. So when he responded with a yes, I couldn't have been more surprised.

"I'm up to try new things," he said. "Let's do it. I should let you go now before you catch a cold out here, but I look forward to trying new things with you, Milena. I'll call you."

And then he was gone as fast as he'd appeared, leaving me to hyperanalyze everything about the conversation that had just taken place.

I finished packing my things and pulled my rain jacket on

over my sweater for the short walk to the car. But even as I was driving away, I couldn't make sense of what had just happened because for the life of me it seemed as if he was flirting with me, and that could never happen because he was a famous model and an almost famous television star.

There was no way he'd be interested in a slightly over-weight, newly licensed real estate agent from Cedar Springs. Not when he could have his pick from the red-carpet beauties.

There was no way.

And there was no way he was ever going to call, so it didn't matter anyway.

Read the rest of One more Moment NOW!

About the Author

Elena Aitken is a USA Today Bestselling Author of more than sixty romance and women's fiction novels. The mother of grown-up twins, Elena now lives with her very own mountain man and two dogs in the heart of the very mountains she writes about. She can often be found with her toes in the lake and a glass of wine in her hand, dreaming up her next book and working on her own happily ever after.

To learn more about Elena:
www.elenaaitken.com
elena@elenaaitken.com